Starfire: Shadow Sun Seven

ALSO BY SPENCER ELLSWORTH

Starfire: A Red Peace

STARFIRE
SHADOW SUN SEVEN

SPENCER ELLSWORTH

A TOM DOHERTY ASSOCIATES BOOK
NEW YORK

This is a work of fiction. All of the characters, organizations, and events portrayed in this novella are either products of the author's imagination or are used fictitiously.

STARFIRE: SHADOW SUN SEVEN

Cover illustration by Sparth
Cover design by Christine Foltzer

Edited by Beth Meacham

A Tor.com Book
Published by Tom Doherty Associates
175 Fifth Avenue
New York, NY 10010

www.tor.com

Tor® is a registered trademark of
Macmillan Publishing Group, LLC.

ISBN 978-0-7653-9574-0 (ebook)
ISBN 978-0-7653-9575-7 (trade paperback)

First Edition: November 2017

For my sisters, with apologies for all the novels you read that I never wrote sequels to. You finally get a Book Two.

"The miracles of the First Empire dumbfound historian and politician both; we look at an era when a Jorian could heal the near-dead, build whole functioning ecospheres and terraform planets in weeks, and we shake our head in disbelief. It creates a climate of fear and reactionism within the Second Empire. We do not trust miracles, for of miracles came devils."

—Thusen Tratus, primary historian of the Order of Saint Thuzera, executed by the Second Empire for high treason in 2IY 946

Entr'acte

She straightened her skirt. It was hot in here. It shouldn't have been. Winter was falling on this part of Irithessa. Cold fog permeated the capital city outside, lay like a shroud over what had been done there.

But then, this capital city felt sealed against the universe. There had been little damage to the inner circle of buildings, and most structures still stood, still filled up with people every day and emptied out every night, despite the fact that the stars above them burned with war.

She looked back at the man across from her.

The new ruler of the galaxy was even more handsome in person than his many, many holos. John Starfire's face was completely unique, a rarity among crosses. A ragged line of salt-and-pepper hair marched across his craggy brow. More covered his jaw. Smile lines and crow's feet framed his eyes, but they didn't soften his hard profile.

It was the kind of face that politicians had custom-shaped, and he had, by all accounts, lucked into it. An accident in the vat that created him. Or so he said.

"I'm sorry," he said, staring out the window past her. "I

don't often sit down."

"I've heard that," she said. "It's all right; you can stand."

Luck gave him the face, but it was not luck that led him to sympathetic media, a string of unlikely victories, and a surprise attack through Irithessa's node. He'd been able to close the nodes to the Dark Zone, trapping the Imperial Navy there, making himself the most formidable military power in the galaxy.

"Tell me your name again."

"Paxin. Paxin sher-Kohin. Not nearly as memorable as John Starfire."

His hand twitched, clenched the sword hilt so tightly his knuckles turned white, released his grip, clenched it again. "Explain to me about this independent agency you belong to, Paxin?"

"Well," she said, starting the same well-rehearsed speech that had gotten her in here, "with all the Imperial screens gone dead in the wake of the, uh, change, we're a new coalition of independent media outlets, and we're seeking the mind of the . . . the new Empire?"

"Not the new Empire," John Starfire said.

"Still the Resistance?"

"We haven't quite figured it out," he said, flashing half of the smile that had won over the galaxy.

"Right. You taking suggestions?"

"What would you suggest?"

"It depends what kind of government you'll practice. A parliamentary system? If so, how tight will be the control? Will it be a loose, confederate group, or ..."

"In these early days, we're remaining focused on consolidation," he said, "since so many systems are falling back on a version of the bluebloods' representative electorate, and we want to show them that such systems must be dismantled."

Translation: *We're going to remain a military occupation as long as we can support it.* And another question she wanted to, but didn't dare ask. *Are you making new crosses in the vats to support your occupation?* He'd promised to stop the vats. Said new crosses would be born by plain old sexual reproduction.

She settled for, "What kind of government are you building exactly, then?"

"Where are you from?" he asked. The smile again.

"People are curious. The Resistance is going from system to system, disassembling the bluebloods' electoral councils and leaving a military occupation. Imperial travel restrictions are still in place, though the Empire is functionally gone. People rely on black markets for world-to-world supplies. All this is ... worrying."

Worrying. One of those words that, in a journalist's hands, was a kind synonym for *Hide everything and run.*

He waited. She kept talking. She would go as long

as he let her. "And then there's the peace with the Dark Zone. You want to talk about any details of that agreement? I mean, how do you even make an agreement with . . . them? How do you even speak?"

"There is peace, and that is what matters." His whole hand turned bloodless from the grip on the sword. "Where are you from?"

"Ah . . . I'm Kerboghan."

"Kerbogha. Interesting world."

"Yes, a couple billion humans, and not a blueblood among us . . ." She realized she had betrayed her species. Until now, he might have guessed she was a cross.

She wasn't stupid. She knew what was happening to humans. "The bluebloods disavowed my people years ago as bastard children. They don't even think we're real humans."

"And what do you believe?" he asked. "Do you think your people are human?"

"This interview should be about you," she said. "Otherwise, I'm just wasting time."

"What are you?"

His eyes burned in the dim light, like twin blue stars. She looked down at her hand terminal, where her notes scrawled across the screen. "A lot of people are curious whether you support any particular creed. You got a lot of support from Biblical congregations."

"I am a Jorian originist," John Starfire said. "You're familiar with the theory?"

She was—that was the notion that the Jorians had actually created life in this galaxy. And there was probably a kernel of truth to it; there were plenty of oxygen-breathing, bipedal species in this galaxy, with anecdotal stories of how they'd crossed at the founding of the First Empire to better unite with the powerful human-Jorian alliance.

The problem was, he didn't believe just the kernel in that truth. He believed the fundamentalist version, in which the Jorians created all life.

"What led you to that belief?"

"If you had seen what I've seen, seen our win against these hopeless odds, you too would realize the nobility of Jorian DNA," he said. "My troops are the true Jorians. I look in their eyes and I know."

Time to switch gears. "How is life with your wife, now that the war is over?"

"She doesn't see much of me," he said. "You are about my daughter's age."

"I didn't know you had children." *That*, the stories left out.

"Four daughters. Three living." He wasn't smiling now.

"I'm sorry."

"My daughter Rashiya was the only one who took after me. The others are happy to be citizens. But Rashiya, she joined the Resistance. She fought. And she died, just a few days ago." He turned back to the window, looked out at the haze over Irithessa's capital city.

"I'm very sorry."

"I know who killed her. That's the thing that gets me." He turned around. "I know it all. Like a play, being acted out on a stage. I can see it all."

"Do you want to talk about—"

"A cross killed her. A cross who knew enough to believe, and yet didn't. How can anyone have so many reasons to believe, see so much, and turn against it?" He shook his head. "He's seen miracles. He's seen us come back from total defeat. And what does this . . . this . . . Araskar take from it?"

"That's his name? Ar . . ."

"Don't write that down."

"Don't worry, ah, I didn't." Her stylus shook. She prided herself on her ability to meet humanoid eyes, to pry answers even from horrific subjects. It was becoming difficult to focus on details, other than that scarred hand clenching and unclenching on that sword hilt. "I think I have enough for the interview."

"You were brave to come here," John Starfire said. "I admire that." He held a hand out to the door.

The door didn't open. Even when she walked within

range, even when she pressed her hand to the pad.

"Unfortunately," John Starfire said, "I am not interested in interviews. I was mostly interested in meeting you, and seeing what sort of human thinks we need an independent press agency. I don't think we do. Not yet, anyway. Not for a few years. We need a firm hand, and the press should be part of that."

"You . . . there has to be freedom on the screens. Even for state-sponsored press," she said. "It's a principle of . . ." She realized she was about to cite the Principles of Empire. The Empire he'd overthrown. She switched tacks. "People supported you because they thought you were fighting for a more just galaxy."

"People get Jorian originism wrong," he said as he walked around the table. "The perception is that we believe humans and Jorians are the only independently evolved species. That's not true. I don't believe that humans evolved. I believe they are merely a bastard species, perhaps made when the Jorians began tinkering to see if they could make weaker, smaller versions of themselves. I like that theory. We've retained several school administrators for the Imperial Academic system who agree with me."

She swallowed the words. *Please let me out.*

"Soon the schools will reopen, and we could invite the media. Even you, as long as this interview meets with the

Resistance's approval. That would be a fine story. Something that plays off people's faith. Not their fear."

She looked right into his smiling eyes and said, "I'm recording this and transmitting it now."

"Who do you think will be brave enough to broadcast it?" he said.

She reached inside herself for the word. "Everyone." She meant to sound defiant, but her voice squeaked.

"When the Vanguard ships hang in orbit above their planet? When they see a planet-cracker blot out the evening stars?" He laughed. "Maybe they'll send someone stronger next time." He stood before her now. "Or perhaps you're stronger than I think. Maybe you simply haven't been tested."

His hand clenched and unclenched on the sword hilt.

-1-

Jaqi

MY LIFE EN'T EVER been simple, but it's been a lot more complicated since I went and did a miracle.

Take this situation, here, right now. I'm at the bottom of a node-relay tower. The node-relay controls communications for this entire moon; it sticks a mile up into the sky, the crystal Jorian structure shining prettily from the middle of a desert junk field, all old chassis and parts, spread out so evil wide it could pass for the Imperial Fleet's secondhand sale.

It's not our node-relay tower; we're hijacking it to try and recruit for the cause. It belongs to the Matakas, the nastiest crime lords on all the nasty worlds, and if they saw what we're doing, they'd kick us out the airlock.

Actually, no airlocks here. We're on the planet surface, where gravity and air are free, so I reckon they'll just fly us evil high and drop us. You'll have to forgive me, as I'm just a spaceways girl.

Yeah, me, Jaqi, the spaceways scab. I am fighting my

own little fight against John Starfire himself, who conquered the galaxy. All because I did a miracle.

Don't ask.

Right now I'm bent over the power cell, greasing it up with anti-oxitate to make sure the thing actually speaks to the tower. Got to grease up the connections before they go back together, as the atmos evil corrodes everything. These power cells work best in vacuum.

"Come on now," I mutter. "Let's get word out to the rest of the galaxy, and get back to camp and eat some real matter." I had tomatoes and corn and beans for breakfast and it was better than anything. 'Cept now I'm ready for lunch. We didn't even eat lunch in the spaceways. It's a noble tradition, lunch. I plan to observe a couple of times a day.

I wipe my hands on my pants, and then see the miracle, looming over me, holding out a handful of sand.

"Here," the miracle says.

"What's this for?"

"It will get the grease off your hands. We often used sand for cleaning, among my people."

"Thanks." I scrub the rough granules across my skin. "Evil rough on the old skin, though." Could use a rag, the kind that we would recycle and re-spin once the fibers got too damaged. But you en't going to be able to keep track of all your rags planetside. (Planetside! Where you can lose things! Did I mention that food grows out of the damn *ground*?)

"You and I have discussed sand before," the miracle says.

"Oh, yeah?"

"Yes." Why's he look so nervous? I en't never seen this slab look nervous. Just cuz I did a miracle? "At the asteroid base. Bill's. We spoke about the relative merits of cleaning with water, sense-field, and sand."

"I remember."

See, the miracle is my friend Z, short for Zaragathora, not that I have any intention of saying that mouthful. He's a Zarra, about seven feet tall and one of those folk your momma warned you about.

Z and I hooked up back on the day the galaxy was "freed." John Starfire, the greatest swordsman and warrior and probably tea-drinker in the galaxy, overthrew the Empire, proclaimed a new order, and then started killing humans. Z and I teamed up to protect a couple of human kids who had a mighty secret, and ran all the way here, to the end of the universe.

Oh, and in the process he died.

And I brought him back to life.

Don't know how. I en't got one little clue.

"What do you suppose it is made of?" Z points up, at the node-relay tower.

I follow his gaze all the way up. Unlike the miles of junk around us, the tower is a Jorian-built relic, so it has the appearance of spun crystal, gleaming and shining with a thousand different colors. Like webs upon webs, spun on top of each other up to the sky.

"Reckon no one knows. Jorian things, left over from the past."

"It is beautiful. It strikes the heart as though the Starfire itself is drawn down from it. A thousand years the galaxy has stood in shadow, and yet the light still offers its mystery."

This is an odd conversation for us, given that this fella knows two words: "blood" and "honor." "You feeling well, Z?"

The handheld comm crackles, and Taltus's snakey voice comes through from above. "I have reached the manual relay screen, sss. Are you hooked up to the cell?"

"Well by."

Taltus, he who's on the other end of this comm, is a big Sska, meaning a lizard, but more important, he is one of them Thuzerians, the military monks what wear the mask and take the vow to protect the innocent. He leads this group of desert runaways, doing everything from gathering seeds to training horses to leading church services. Now he reckons I should talk to his preaching heads. "Everything running smooth, sss? We must have uninterrupted connection with the Council of Elders."

"Evil smooth, aiya. You sure these folk'll hear you?"

"I have invoked the great blood oath, most sacred to God. They must. For you, the Son of Stars, call them."

"Uh . . ." How's a girl supposed to answer that? "Yeah."

The power hums, all juiced-up on solar cells. In space, you can draw power off background radiation, when you pass through a heavy belt, or just burn unthunium, but there en't none of that planetside. Just go ahead and grab some of that sunlight, we do.

I scan the horizon. No trouble coming from beyond this junkyard. Not yet, anyway. The folk what went out to serve as a distraction must have worked.

I walk over to check on the kids, what got me into all this trouble to start with. They squat next to the power cell, looking at the horizon—well, the little boy, Toq, does. The girl, Kalia, is a bit more interested in the older boy next to her.

Erdo is one of the random desert kids we've all been breaking bread with for the last couple of weeks. And he's a classic scab. Stolen more than he's ever owned, survived off protein packs, and ended up here after a job gone south. He's got a year on Kalia, is tall and quick-spoken, with a ragged crop of hair. Kalia's flush as five suns for him.

"She said it wasn't worth a shit in space," Kalia giggles.

"Oh, aiya, it en't, trust me," the boy says. "When I worked the spaceways, we woulda had power cells three times this size." He gives a grin and tosses his hair, as if this power cell is a thing to brag about—to a blueblood like Kalia! "You shoulda seen one I took off a scow near Routalais. Could power a whole ecosphere."

"Wow," Kalia says.

Then he sees me and he and Kalia both look at me strange—Kalia because she's a girl been caught going flush over a boy, but Erdo—well, this little spaceways scab of a boy hops to his feet and *bows*.

The bowing again. "Don't do that," I say.

He don't listen. Comes up out of the bow graceful as a fine servant in a holo. "Message for the sentries, ah, Saint Jaqi?"

"Erdo, stop that." I done explained it lots of times. "Taltus told you. I en't no Saint. It don't work like that."

"Yeah," Kalia butts in. "Saints have to perform three witnessed miracles. Jaqi's just done one."

That don't help. "I didn't do a thing. You stop that bowing."

Erdo nods, hair flopping around on his little head. "I'll go tell the guards, Saint—ma'am."

"Ma'am?" I can't help laughing at the poor kid. "Ma'am! That's even worse!"

Erdo starts to say something again, but sputters, and

seems to think better of it. He leaves to speak with the sentries.

These folk.

They were fine the first week or so. The kindest wanderers you could imagine, all of them with a similar story—they run from trouble elsewhere in the galaxy, and those of them who heard about our trouble were kind. We didn't speak on the trouble unless asked, and that was well by me. But then word of what I done with Z got around, and one day they start bowing, and calling me Saint.

"Oh, my gosh, Jaqi," Kalia groans once her boy is out of earshot. "You don't have to insult people's faith!"

"When did I insult anyone's faith? And who's gosh?"

"People believe in you," she says, like this is something everyone knows. "Ever since you brought Z back to life, people see you as someone to look up to. That's only going to increase the longer we're fighting against John Starfire."

"Yeah, well, folk ought to put their faith in something a bit more reliable."

"What's more reliable than a miracle we witnessed with our own eyes?" She turns to her brother. "Right, Toq?"

"I want Erdo to take me on a horse again," Toq answers. Unlike his sister, Toq is young enough not to make too much of a fuss.

"Toq, you don't think it's crazy to believe Jaqi can do miracles, right? We saw her bring Z back to life."

"Yeah," Toq says. And with all the energy of a kid, he adds, "You are gonna kill John Starfire!"

"Let's talk about something else."

"Just because you don't know how you did it," Kalia says, "that's no reason not to try and figure it out—"

Just then the comm crackles, saving me. "Losing power," Taltus says. "Check the relay orientator, please. Where is Araskar? I need to speak to him."

I walk over to where our independent power cell's been patched into the tower, through several wires fed into a relay orientator. Araskar's bent over it.

Araskar.

My crew is a funny bunch. Bluebloods on one hand, pit-fighting Zarra on the other. A religious type or two.

But Araskar is the most crazing slab in all the spaceways.

Up until we made planetfall, he tried to kill us. He was part of that Vanguard that chased us halfway across the galaxy, targeted the kids for murder, and invaded Bill's, my home. He only decided to join us at the last of all possible moments, when he turned around and killed his buddy what was about to cut down Kalia.

Goes without saying that I don't trust him no further

than the end of a soulsword.

All that said . . . he is a grade-A slab.

He's only wearing a pair of shorts and his scarred skin is even darker brown than usual, and as he hunches over the power cell I see (oh, do I evil see) the way those scar-laced muscles contract from years of training and soldiering.

I can't help thinking that we're both crosses, and if he gave me the slack, everything would work as intended. It would be a right old time.

See, these en't the thoughts of no Saint!

"You need something?" he asks.

"Taltus wants your ear." I hand the comm over. Araskar and Taltus talk back and forth, Araskar tweaking levels on the orientator. "That should do it," Araskar says into the comm. "Try it now."

"Receiving," Taltus says, his voice muffled by that mask all of his Order wears. We wait, and I try not to let Araskar see how I'm regarding him, a mixture of side-eye for his crazing, and appreciation for his chest.

"Any answer from your people?" Araskar says to the comm.

Taltus's voice crackles through the comm. "It will take time, sss. I have spoken to one lower Adept."

"What'd you do to get kicked out of this Order, anyway?" I ask.

"We had a doctrinal disagreement, sss." Taltus cuts off the comm signal, like he always does when I bring this up.

I turn back to Araskar, and for lack of anything to say, offer, "No sign of trouble yet."

He puts his hand on the sword at his side, maybe without realizing it. "I'm ready."

"What's that thing going to do?" I point to the sword. "Them Kurguls don't swing swords. They just turn you into shard-food." I know what this fellow is thinking. "You going to go get yourself dead? You promised not to. You gonna learn guitar."

"I didn't promise anything," he says, surly as ever, "but I'm not going to get myself killed. Although life won't be worth much if the Thuzerians won't help us."

"So optimistic there, fella."

"Just realistic." He squints at me, shading his eyes, looking at the horizon. I don't see no dust out there, but I en't never been in a big wide-open planet space anyway. "There are only a few major military powers in the galaxy, and the military monks are the only ones who never pledged to the Resistance or the Empire."

"Don't sound so fatal, slab! We got a chance of recruiting some folk to our . . . what'd you call it."

"Counter-resistance."

"That's a terrible name."

"You're welcome to come up with something better." He turns back to the orientator, like it needs his attention. "Nothing will matter if we can't learn what John Starfire knows about the Dark Zone. Why it mattered that the kids had that memory crypt."

He's talking about the map we saw, afore we made planetfall here. Evil big map of stars, all the stars swallowed by the Dark Zone way back when. I don't like thinking about that Dark Zone. Don't like thinking about the cold, that sick little half-light, about a face the size of a planet, a face that could swallow whole suns. I accidentally jumped in there and got enough for a lifetime. "You, uh, you know anything about them devils?"

"No more than you. A thousand years ago, the Shir—"

"Aiya, slab! Don't name the devil!"

He laughs, without humor. Told you this fellow was crazing. "All right, a thousand years ago *they* appeared, at the same time the Jorians disappeared. *They* killed a thousand star systems, swallowing suns to burn *their* internal furnaces, before the Imperial Navy was formed to stop *them,* with the first successful cross soldiers. But that's just propaganda I got in my data dump. Along with *You Are the Hero the Empire Needs Now* and *Battle: The Purpose of Cross Life* and *Understanding Sentience: A Primer for Non-Sentient Races.*" He laughs, but it en't a happy laugh. I don't think he knows how to do a happy laugh. "I don't know any of the real history from that time. What little information is left is in the memory crypts, or . . ." He pauses.

"Or what?"

"Or somewhere no one can find it."

This is the way he goes. If he didn't drive me so mad with his crazing, I'd be worried about him pulling out that sword to use on himself. "Don't sound so sad about things. Think about your guitar. Think about lunch. Just don't spend too much time thinking on the dead, aiya?"

I try to make myself sound friendly. By his scowl and narrowed eyes, I failed. "What do you know?" He turns back to me, them cold eyes surrounded by them scars, and I remember, again, that this slab is a killer, moreso than even Z. "You don't even understand who you are, or what you did back there. I killed the woman I loved because of you. I—" He cuts himself off.

"Well, that's some honesty there. Don't stop! What else you going to say? That I ought to know how I did a damn miracle? Because I would damn well like to know, slab!"

He turns back to the horizon, doesn't answer me.

"You had the idea. You said you heard music coming off me."

"Yes," he says, hardly without opening his lips.

"Magic music, miracle stuff that makes me some kinda special."

"Yes. I hear it all the time. I hear it right now. I don't have an explanation for it."

"But you just looked at me back there, and you saw Z laid out all dead, and you thought, oh, hey, I ought to have her use that music to bring this slab back to life—that's what you thought? All from one look?"

"No, I knew something was special about you. For a long time."

"What? When? When did we ever chat before this, slab?"

"At the asteroid base. I was in one of the Moths that attacked you. I could hear the music then."

The base.

Bill's.

My home.

The home the Vanguard waltzed in and smashed up, and though I killed a good number of them, enough got through that they killed Bill, who was a father to me after my parents died. Then they nearly killed the kids, and poisoned Z. "You knew I was special back at Bill's."

His scars contort with confusion. "What's Bill's?"

"The asteroid." Now it's my turn to sound cold. "You knew I was special, and you tried to kill me anyway, and let them folk kill my own?"

"It wasn't like that. I—"

"You hadn't figured this business out, then."

He pauses. "No. Not yet."

"Just figured I was special, not figured the Resistance was evil for wanting to kill kids."

"It was complicated."

"Sure it was." I'm so angry I could say a thousand things at once, and nothing at all. "Sure it was. I mean, in the spaceways, someone tries to kill young ones, they have a happy accident with an airlock. But it's more complicated with all your learning. How many Imperial years you seen, now? One? Or you fresher from the vat than that?"

"I'm five years out of the vat," he says.

"So much wisdom in them five years. So much *complication*."

He stares at me for a long time, and his hand twitches on the smaller of the two swords he wears, like he's about to yank it out and start a fight. "I told you. I was wrong. The Resistance was wrong."

"Lot of folk 'wrong' is gonna bring back, slab—"

A shard flies right past us and explodes, blowing an old ship's engine housing into a thousand white-hot fragments, spinning through the air.

"Matakas!"

Shit.

"Thought we sent out a diversion!" A bunch of desert folk went to hit the Matakas' storehouse not five miles away, precisely so we could do this.

"They weren't fooled," Araskar says. "Or they've got enough drones to deal with both threats."

I drop, crawl along the sand on my elbows, gun in one hand. The power cell is the big worry here—they hit that, and we lose communication, and we get an evil explosion and some toxic radiation to spare, given all stored in them batteries. My gun hums with shards, the same nice vintage Zarronen I been carrying since I met the kids. "Where are they?"

Araskar draws his sword and runs out into the open. I half expect him to vanish in a hail of shard-fire, but he outruns each red gleam, dances between bits of junk.

"Kids!" I run toward where I left Kalia and Toq. They was just on the other side of the power cell, against the tower, but they en't there now.

The comm chooses that minute to buzz. The entire node-relay tower crackles, and the spun-crystal turns bright blue, patterns of blue twisting and spinning along its whole length. The blue light is even brighter than the sunlight, washing me in shades of blue, washing the whole shard-happy junkyard in blue.

"Jaqi, sss." Taltus's lizard voice hisses through the comm. "I have reached the elders of my Order. They wish to speak with you, to determine whether you are truly the one prophesied—"

More junk blows up, on the other side of the tower from me. "Evil busy over here!"

"Is this the girl?" A deep voice comes through the comm. "This is Father Abodus, head of the Council of Saint Thuzera—"

I still can't see the kids. I bolt from the side of the power cell through the dirt, keeping low. Kids probably took off into the junkyard. That would be the worst thing to do, as it puts them right out there in the dangerous shrapnel, and makes them an easier target.

I run from one piece of junk to the next, from the burnt-out engine of a Keil Spinner X5 to the still half-decent chassis of a Z-Nova J-26.

That low voice rumbles from the comm. "How will you destroy the Shir?"

"What?" They really just ask me that?

"Tell us how you will destroy the Shir! The Son of Stars must conquer the devil, and bring light unto the darkened stars—"

A couple of explosions in the distance. "The special oogie of space en't got a clue about that, and don't name the devil," I mutter, but I think the comm picks it up, because they say a few other things I lose in the process of running.

"Jaqi, sss!" There's Taltus, shouting now. "Please, speak to my elders. I cannot maintain the faster-than-light connection for long. Please, sss, tell them something."

I duck behind a piece of machinery, hating everything in the galaxy, especially them prophecies, that Bible, and bowing most of all. I yell into the comm, "I don't know how to stop them devils, but I reckon the first step is stopping John Starfire, ai? He's the only one talked to them and come out alive!"

The crackle of the node-relay comes through and I hear that same deep voice. "How did you perform this miracle?"

Another explosion, too close, spattering me with bits of machine and sand. I wipe sand out of my eyes. "Uh, there's a sort of music, and I reckon it's like the Starfire, and I used a sword to put the music inside a fella and he came back to life."

"Music."

"Aiya. I mean yes." Come on, talk like fancy folk, Jaqi, not like a scab!

"You used a sword to—"

"Give me that."

A Mataka drone stands not three paces off me.

He glares through little black eyes, rattling his vestigial wings inside his carapace, like they do when they're excited. His tentacles quiver, hanging off his face. He's got a gun—a piece of crap knockoff Keil—trained on my head.

"Give me that comm."

I fake my best swindler smile. "You really going to shoot me with that garbage? I reckon the shard makes it halfway out before it blows your hand off. Now this—this is a piece." I hold up my gun. "You take it, I keep the comm, aiya?"

"You are truly the stupidest female I have ever——" A red flash, and suddenly this Kurgul is smeared a good forty feet across the desert.

Z comes running across the desert at me. "I am sorry, I should have seen you before!" he snarls.

"En't no thing, thank you—wait, did you just say you was *sorry*?"

Them tattoos on his cheek twist up in a more complicated version of his usual frown. "Yes."

Next, Araskar's gonna kiss me. I thumb the comm. "Okay, where were—"

And the blue light vanishes.

Either Taltus lost the connection to my handheld comm, or the Matakas figured it out and killed the faster-than-light node-relay from the master satellites in orbit. "Well, I hope I impressed them folk," I say, knowing I did the opposite.

"The children," Z says.

"Kalia!" I see her and Erdo, running across the desert, trying to make it to cover behind some of the junk. "Don't go—"

Too late. One of them hoverbugs has noticed those kids. It roars across the sand toward us, waves of force from the sense-field underneath it knocking the machinery aside.

Z and I open up on the hoverbug. I loose quite a few decent shots, one of which hits the back of the hoverbug, sends it into a spin. Z spends his shots on the sense-field in the front.

"You en't much of a shot, Z—"

"There is no honor in this!"

They let out a barrage at us, and we both drop to the sand. The hoverbug spins, clips the chassis of an old ship, and goes flying through the air and wrecks against another stripped ship frame.

I go running to the kids.

It's just Kalia and Erdo, both of them clinging to each other. I turn to Z. "You hid Toq somewhere safe?"

"I did not see him, by blood and honor! I have not seen the youngest boy since we arrived at the tower."

"Where is he?" I look at Kalia.

"I don't know!" she says. "He went looking for you, just before they attacked—"

Z doesn't hesitate—he lopes off right away to find Toq.

I grab Kalia, pull her close into an embrace. "You well?"

"I'm okay," Kalia says, feeling her chest and her legs and arms. "I'm—I'm not even singed." She turns to the boy with all the simple concern of a girl flush for a boy. "I—Erdo, are you okay?"

Erdo looks at me, looks at her, flips his hair a bit again, and bows.

"None of—"

He keeps bowing. Falls right over, exposing where a huge chunk of glowing shrapnel's embedded in his back.

"Oh shit!" I thumb the comm for a local signal. "Taltus, get down here, we need someone knows their medical!" I grab Erdo, try to lay him out—he's limp as a dead freighter and his eyes glassy, and now I can see how much blood's poured down his pant legs. A lot. Burning hell and the devil. I never seen so much blood.

I try not to think it, but I do. Just like Quinn. Another kid dying here, in my arms, another kid didn't do anything wrong but get mixed up with the wrong folk. I hardly know a thing about this kid. All I know is that he bows. And bleeds.

"He's going to die." I said it out loud. Not again. I promised myself no more.

"Jaqi, no, wait." Kalia puts her hand on mine. "You have to heal him, Jaqi."

"I what?"

"You have to heal him! Like you did Z! Just do it again!"

I look back behind us, in front of us, like Araskar's going to appear from wherever he run off to. "I en't got the sword this time," I say, sounding like the fool I am.

"Just—just do what you did! Channel the Starfire! Heal him! You did it before!"

"I did, didn't I?" Still sound like a fool. "I—" Okay, Jaqi, this boy's bleeding out in front of you. You done this before. Where's that music? I thought about my mother before, thought about them field songs she sung. Just a simple beat. *Bend, pull, bend, pull.* So's I start to sing it.

"Bend, pull, take the weed, bend, pull, take the weed . . ." I don't remember any other words, but I reckon there was some, so I stop and think and Kalia yells, "Jaqi!"

"Oops, I mean, bend, pull, music, come on music, come on, come . . ." Where's the music? Where's them big, sweeping songs coming out of the stars? "Any minute now, bend, pull . . ." I don't hear a thing but the wind and the buzz of other hoverbugs.

Erdo gives a twitch, then dies in my miracle-working arms.

-2-

Araskar

IN THE STOLEN MEMORY, my stubble tickles Rashiya's cheek. She clings to my neck, her breasts pressed against my scarred back. I smell of sweat and stale spaceship. Her chin nests on my shoulder while we both read the comic book.

On the comic book page, Scurv Silvershot takes a drag off his cigarette, raises his gun, and fires one last shot. The drawn shard arcs through space, through miles of vacuum, and hits another character and produces a cascade of poorly colored blood, the wound gushing in lovingly rendered pen-and-ink detail—

She puts a finger to the word bubbles. The garish page of Scurv Silvershot comic book ripples under her hand. "Finding some wisdom?" she says. She's never met another soldier who collects comic books. She rather likes them.

"Look at that."

On the faded page, the wounded character bleeds out

poorly colored blood, and Scurv Silvershot stands over him, Scurv's jutting chin filling the comic panel.

"Read it to me," Rashiya says.

"So right here, Scurv Silvershot's partner is talking. He says, 'Remember on the Omnitron, when we stole the memories of a thousand worlds? Remember what you said?' And Scurv Silvershot answers, and shoots his buddy in the head to make it quick. 'That I do, partner. Memory's blade cuts deepest of all.'"

"Good wisdom in the comic books," Rashiya says. "Why'd he have to shoot the guy?"

"Betrayal," I say.

And that breaks the spell of the memory.

My vision reshapes into Jaqi, staring at me, her dark skin and braided hair covered in dust and sweat, her eyes narrowed, her hand twitching angrily. Music rolls off her, a restrained, low pulse of percussion under a furious stringed instrument. "So much wisdom in those five years."

The word *wisdom* spreads out from her in a rush of music, three repeated notes with a swirl of tones sustaining them, harmonizing with Rashiya's sentence. These memories wash over me whenever I don't expect it.

"So much *complication*."

My hand strays to my short soulsword, clutches the handle. *Here, Jaqi. Here's some wisdom. Memory's blade cuts deepest of all.*

I see what I could do, like it's a memory I haven't earned—or stolen—yet. I could take the short sword out. Stab it right into my arm—not too deep, just enough to part the skin, to send a steady flow of dark blood into the crook of my elbow, turn to white fire and blaze up the blade of the sword—and suck up the memories.

Forget my friends, turned to meat in the hallway of an Imperial dreadnought, forget my slugs, turned into space debris by Jaqi. Forget the pills, pink dots sitting on my callused palm, all the times I swallowed my doubts about the Resistance with those pills. Forget the horrible wrench in my hand, when my soulsword stabbed the woman I loved. She was a monster. She was trying to kill a child. I still loved her.

I'm past wanting to kill myself. I'm fine with living, as long as they'll let me forget.

I asked. Asked Taltus, as he seemed removed from the whole thing. *We cannot let you forget, sss. You are the key, Araskar, with the intel you took from John Starfire's daughter.* I asked the Zarra. *There is no honor in forgetting.*

I don't care. I can't live another day with these memories.

Jaqi is staring. I clear my throat. "I told you. I was wrong. The Resistance was wrong."

"Lot of folk 'wrong' is gonna bring back, slab—"

Shards fly past Jaqi and I.

Thank the Starfire. I unsheathe my proper soulsword, made for offense, and slash my arm.

White fire springs up the blade.

I grab my armor-shirt and helmet where I've left them on the sand, throw them on. Here I am in the Vanguard's armor again. Hopefully I'll die in it this time.

The Mataka hoverbugs roar, circling the junkyard. Shards flash, red-and-white trails across my vision, contrasting with the sudden blue of the lit-up node tower.

One of the hoverbugs kicks up its heavy thrusters, and flies up the side of the tower. I run into the open to distract them, so they won't kill poor Taltus.

Shards come flashing red at me. One whistles past my leg. One past my head, close enough to burn off hair. I dodge between bits of space junk, even though a shard isn't a bad way to die, with a direct hit. A small shard pings off my soulsword. Around me, the junk explodes. Metal chunks and splinters fly through the air in bursts, rain down on me, but despite all the white-hot metal in the air, my Vanguard armor holds.

Bleeding out here would be a lousy death. Although it wouldn't take too long, if I lost the right limb.

I drop, roll behind some wreckage, and wait for the hoverbug chasing me to fly over me. I jab up, slice its fuel line, yank the soulsword down just fast enough to keep it from being pulled out of my hand.

The hoverbug spins, knocking divots out of the dirt, and wrecks into the side of the tower, scattering junk and Kurgul drone bits all across the landscape.

I sheathe my sword, grab a strut of the tower, and climb up a good hundred feet, fast as I can.

The female Zarra in our desert crew stands on one of the tower platforms, firing down at the climbing Kurgul drones, picking them off. We call her X, as her real name's a mouthful.

She sees me and nearly shoots, only stopping just in time. Her tattooed face twisted into a familiar grimace. "Araskar! Aid me!" She tosses me her rifle.

I catch the rifle. It displays a blinking yellow light. "This is empty!"

She smiles, because Zarra are insane, and draws a long knife and a sense-rope. "A fine club, no? Blood and honor!"

A hoverbug rises to the left of me, drones yelling insults as they prime more shards in the big gun mounted to its front, ready to blow us right off the tower.

I leap from the node-relay tower to the hoverbug, the distance yawning beneath my feet, and suddenly I'm standing on the hood of the hoverbug, looking down the barrel of this mounted rail gun, holding a much smaller gun, losing my balance, my gun entirely out of shards, so

I shove my empty rifle down the rail gun's barrel—

The explosion throws me back against the tower. Lucky for me the shard load itself blows out the back of the rail gun, breaks the hoverbug apart, just giving me a blast of white-hot shrapnel that embeds itself in my armor—except I fall, grabbing for a spar of the tower, and I miss and falling might just be how I die—

A sense-rope catches my ankle, the glowing white length lifting me back up. X pulls my singed self up to the platform.

Not dead yet.

Thick, tattooed Zarra arms lift me over the edge. "Do not be so quick to die!" She spits out the words at me, and slaps my helmet. "There is no honor in avoidable death!"

"You're welcome," I croak. My ribs ache from the hit against the side of the tower, and the shrapnel embedded in my armor burns, even through the high-impact fiber.

"I too have lost honor, coming to this moon," she says, like she's explaining something to a child. "It pains me greatly, every day. But a quick, foolish death will not restore you in the eyes of the ancestors. Only blood and honor go with you to the River of Stars, where the ancestors wait."

"I don't have any ancestors," I say.

"That is a great tragedy. Had I time, I would sing a

mourning song. Go assist Taltus with his machinery."

I climb up to Taltus, one crystalline platform above. Sska tend to be short, but Taltus is some kind of genetic mutant. He's massive, even taller than Z. The bone-mask, sign of his Order, sits crookedly on his face, showing hints of the scaly features beneath. He wields a soulsword very different from mine, a massive, T-hilt broadsword, a black-bladed thing sprouting blue fire. Thuzerian soulswords are forged by hand. Unlike our psychic resonators, theirs are supposed to work entirely on faith.

He's frantically punching the display of the screen that interfaces with the node-relay, trying to reestablish contact. "She was going to tell them! Tell them how to save all the stars, to end the thousand-year darkness, end their retreat and stand, and I could come back to the Order—"

"I don't think Jaqi was going to say all that," I mutter, slumping to the ground. I reach for the water on my belt.

My fingers meet a huge hole in the metal of the bottle. A piece of shrapnel has robbed me of my water. Damn it.

I hear a rush of music, high dissonant notes. My head jerks of its own volition, to look down. "Jaqi's in trouble." Taltus follows my gaze, to see a Kurgul with a gun trained on Jaqi.

"The Son of Stars!"

"I'll keep an eye on this," I say. "Go help her."

Taltus climbs down. I pick up his screen and try

punching a code, to get the transmission back—and then another hoverbug rises up behind me. I whirl around, armed only with my soulswords, pretty sure I'm finally going to die, thank God—

A Mataka drone, this one with a wide-brimmed hat pulled low, sits in the gunner chair of this hoverbug, holding Toq, a gun pointed at the kids' head. Toq cries. The Mataka in the hat shakes the kid. "Put down the sword, or I see if this kid can fly."

I hesitate. The soulsword feels good in my hand. This would be a good place to die.

"Come on, Araskar," the drone says, addressing me by name. "You're the big payday. Don't you want to take the heat off the others?"

A drone hops from the hoverbug, holds up a pair of manacles. I sigh, and hand the swords to the drone.

Still not dead yet.

The ocean coast of the moon of Trace is lovely. Grassy green hills as far as the eye can see, dotted with clumps of red-barked trees. Fluted, spun-glass Jorian towers atop those hills. Deep, rushing rivers and babbling streams fill the bottomlands. If I didn't have a gun in my back I'd take a picture.

Of course, the Kurguls tend to ruin everything they touch. Take the Jorian ruins we're piloting toward. A couple of the airy, crystalline structures catch the light of Trace's sun, reflecting off Trace itself, the glowing Suit planet that takes up half the sky. It should be gorgeous, the sun and the illuminated curve of the planet reflected a thousand times through the Jorian architecture. But the light-catching towers all are bedecked with enormous globs of Kurgul nest, like leaking bubbles of pus.

Smoke pours out of the holes in the nests, mars what little light comes through the structures. The nests are made up mostly of secretion from the nest queen, whatever twigs and rocks are handy. And pieces of dead Kurguls. We circle a giant pustule of nest, made of thousands of arms, heads and bits of exoskeleton glued together, the innards having been cleaned out.

"You sure know how to ruin a view," I say.

A drone shoves a hot shard-barrel against my cheek, burning it, the heat aching in my teeth, then kicks me in the stomach. "Don't talk, cross."

When we land, the Matakas shove us out of their hoverbug at gunpoint, up the walkway.

They haul X out of another hoverbug, manacled and covered in far more burns and cuts than me. "You dare use a child to manipulate your enemies—your shame is compounded to the stars, you are—"

"Shut up already." They prod her with a shock stick, and she falls over, lurching into me, all seven feet of her. I'm unable to catch my balance with my hands bound, so down we both go. Ow. I hurt enough already.

"Easy!" I groan, from underneath X. "I have a plan! Easy!"

"Blood and honor," she snarls, but rolls off me and lets the drones pull her to her feet, then stands there unmoving until one jabs her with the shock stick again.

We walk through a smoky hallway, choking and coughing, under bits of carapace, severed heads, and lots of little spindly Kurgul arms mixed in with the cement and the sticks in the walls. The whole species crossed about a thousand years ago to stop a population crisis and ended up with a surplus of drones. Even now, nest queens should give birth to mostly workers, but their eggs are sixty percent angry, touchy, crime-hungry drone. Drones deemed useless get turned into infrastructure.

"Don't worry, kid," I say, leaning toward Toq in the shackles that bind my entire arms. Far away, the music spirals up, notes upon notes, letting me know Jaqi is worried about this kid. "I'm a good talker."

"What if they don't listen?"

"Kurguls always listen. You offer them a better deal, they can't help but take it." I don't mention that I may not actually have the better deal. Kid's reassured, right?

That's what matters?

He starts crying.

So, not reassured. Give me a break; everyone I know was born an adult.

Then he wipes the tears on his upper arm, moving his manacled arms as much as he can get away with, and says, "Really?"

"Soldier's honor."

Please don't ask what a soldier's honor is actually worth, kid.

They pull open a couple of ancient Jorian doors, wide and round, fine crystal webs studded with gobs of Kurgul secretion.

The nest queen of the Matakas stands on the other side, on a dais made of dead drones, her wide-padded feet propped up on staring severed, eyeless heads.

She could almost pass for a worker Kurgul, but more stocky and thick-set than the small figures that scurry around her. A large, sticky belly juts from her middle, glistening with royal jelly. Unlike the drones, with their black eyes, face tentacles, and little sucking mouths, she's got a wide head with thick mandibles that shine in the dim light that comes through the crystal overhead. Behind her sits a distended and swollen egg sac, taking up most of the dais.

About ten thousand new Matakas in there.

Machinery takes up much of the dais as well, a forest of wires feeding into the egg sac. Unlike the bluebloods, and most religions of the galaxy, Kurguls embrace the act of crossing. The nest queens like the competition among their drones. They monitor the genetic mix and harvest from the best genes they can find to make their next batch all the more ambitious, evolving with each generation.

Swez approaches the dais and bows, then is allowed to walk up the steps made of the dismembered bodies of his brothers, and he is allowed to take one solitary lick of the nest queen's belly.

After that, her workers grab him and toss him down the steps. He rolls downstairs over bits of exoskeleton, crawls back to his knees, and continues to genuflect.

Kurguls are weird.

She barks something at Swez and he answers back—and I understand it! "Egg-layer, I have given you a key to undo our nest's shame."

I speak Kurgul? I guess I must. Got it with the data dump, when I came out of the vats.

Cross brains are built to have a kind of recall most sentient minds can't evolve, and along with my standard Imperial propaganda data dump (the highlight was *It Doesn't Matter Whether You're Sentient or Not*) when I came out of the vats, it seems I got Kurgul.

Knowledge filters in. Any interaction between the nest queen and the drones can be considered part of the courtship ritual. If I keep letting Swez speak for me, I'll look like the weakest worker in their hive. Or worse, a disgraced drone. I can use the generic pronouns for a foreigner, but Kurguls don't like being referred to as foreigners in their own language.

A worker's pronouns and tenses are entirely subservient. I don't want that.

So a drone I must be.

Which means, by default, I'll sound like I'm bidding to mate.

Only a week after I killed my last girlfriend. Way to move on, Araskar.

"Egg-layer," I say, using the pronoun a drone does.

Swez brings up the shock stick, but the queen barks a command and he stops.

"Wingless one," the queen replies. She's referring to me as a beaten drone, one she's about to rip apart and weave into the infrastructure of their home.

Not a good start.

"Wingless one? I killed three of your drones and was not mutilated, egg-layer."

"They have your wings," she says, and two long antennae unfurl from her head to point at the drones who hold my soulswords, at the back of the chamber.

I laugh. "I'm not crippled without those. Come now, egg-layer. Let me into your dais." Once again, as a worker, I would ask to *approach* the dais. Makes me feel like I need a slick-down soundtrack and a few open clasps on my shirt.

She unfurls one of her antennae, strokes her long swollen pupator. "Why does John Starfire have your face smeared on every screen in the wild worlds?"

"I killed his daughter."

She makes a noise that I suspect is a Kurgul sigh. "Why do some sentients care so much for spawn? If his child fell in battle, then her genes were too weak to continue."

"Egg-layer, I have come through thousands of battles. I stood in the smoke of Irithessa's great pyramids. I have battled the galaxy's great drone, John Starfire." Well, close enough. "I come here with an offer."

"An offer? An offer better than what John Starfire offers for you?" Her mandibles twist as if they're looking to grab something. "I'm about to see whether the Chosen One will take a cross without even half a tongue."

"The Resistance is broke." I enunciate every word. There's nice ways to ask someone to speak clearly, but Matakas don't know that. "Now that shouldn't surprise you, as we were always living off charity. Funny thing is, once we got into power, we found out the Empire was broke, too."

Swez's shock stick hums, but the nest queen gurgles at him, and, surprising everyone, he puts it down.

"You think I am too proud to take a letter of credit, wingless?"

"A Hukas letter of credit?"

Wings rattle all over the chamber and the queen hisses. "What's this about Hukas?" Hukas are the Kurgul nest all the other nests love to hate. The richest, most decadent nest, funding most illegal activity in the galaxy, squeezing out minor, angry nests like the Matakas.

"The Hukas are the only reliable investors in the brave new galaxy, egg-layer. The Resistance is ears-deep in debt to them."

A whole chorus of angry vestigial wings rattles around the room.

"Egg-layer, you can lick the Hukas' bellies for the next ten years, if you want." Half the drones reach for their guns, and the nest queen doesn't stop them. She hisses, a really horrible rattling hiss that I'm sure means I am about to die. But then she speaks.

"Offer me something better, wingless, or I rip out the rest of your tongue."

I close my eyes and let words filter out of Rashiya's memories. "Shadow Sun Seven. You know it?"

"No, wingless."

Swez speaks up. "Seen the inside of two Shadow Suns. Corporate prisons."

"Seven *was* a prison. Since the fall of the Empire, it's been a center for pit fights. Lots of money changing hands. Lots of important prisoners."

"Why so much money in a prison?"

"Because this Shadow Sun is located in the cleared-out guts of a Ruuzan Threg." I have the queen's attention now. "You know what those are, don't you?"

The queen nods to Swez and Swez says, "Air-sucking space ticks. Used in the Andelaxan War."

"Andelaxan pirates used them to get all the oxygen and moisture out of a ship in minutes," I say. "Fly up to the side of an Imperial cruiser, have the Threg pierce its hull, and the oxygen is gone in minutes, stored and conveniently reusable. Once the Empire beat the pirates, they turned the oxygen mines into prisons. That means Shadow Sun Seven has enough hyperdense cells to make the Matakas the most wealthy nest in the galaxy."

Swez snorts, a fake laugh if I've ever heard one.

But the nest queen gives me an appreciative gurgle, and every drone in the room stops rattling their wings.

I keep going. "Real matter. Value in hand. No letters of credit, no bowing to the Hukas."

The nest queen speaks. "And you cased this station?"

"I didn't. But I just stabbed someone who did." I nod

toward the soulsword, in the hand of two drones at the back of the room. "You give me a complement of drones, we'll bring a load of hyperdense cells back. Imagine the bartering power that gives you."

The drones start rattling wings, and Swez looks ready to speak, but the nest queen cuts him off by speaking to me. "Well-spoken, wide-thorax."

Well. She's now referring to me with the pronouns one would use for an attractive drone.

"This will be our deal. Matter in hand. You will provide the way in, we will provide ships and drones for your use."

"A fine decision," I say, over the discontented rattling of Swez's wings.

The nest queen notices her drones' discontent, and lets out another rattling hiss. "I will not lick a Hukas belly! Silence, or become wingless yourself. I need material to build larval chambers."

When Swez does speak, my data dump lets me know that the particular thrum in his vestigial wings means *humble*. "Egg-layer, what will you do with . . . the cross?"

"Wide-thorax here will become part of our lineage."

"Uh." Searching through my memory of the Kurgul language, I'm not finding any words to respectfully decline mating with her. They just . . . don't exist. A drone doesn't refuse the queen.

"Come here, wide-thorax," she says. "Partake."

Two drones force me up the dais. Dead drone bodies crunch under my feet. They bend me down, as if I couldn't figure it out, to lick the glistening jelly off the nest queen's belly.

Royal jelly oozes out of holes like pores across the wide yellow spread of soft flesh, the only soft flesh I've seen on a Kurgul.

Memories of Rashiya intrude, and I shut my eyes, as if that'll help. Memories of kissing, of undressing her. Memories of her skin, touching mine. Memories of her skin, drained of memories and dead.

Memories of her speaking to her father.

In the memory, John Starfire looks back across the node-relay screen. Hair going white, smile lines at the edge of his eyes.

"Let's talk your next mission, Rash," her father says. "You get that memory-crypt from the kids, and then a pickup. Should be straightforward, unless the prison warden gives you trouble."

"What's this about prison, pater?" Rashiya asks. She's trying not to show how tired she is. Or show that she doesn't agree with her father's assessment of Araskar. She doesn't think I'll be loyal.

"Keep this one to yourself. There's someone imprisoned on Shadow Sun Seven, Rash. I need you to get them out, after you've finished with the children."

Rashiya is not happy. "The prison? That place has gone wild. I had enough trouble with the scabs on the last place you sent me."

He ignores "Memorize these schematics. You should be able to do a requisition—the warden owes me—but if he gives you trouble, it's not too hard to shoot your way in if needed."

"Why is this prisoner so important?"

And then, as usual the memory of my own sword slamming through her chest, and that sudden tight pain, that inability to breathe, that surprise. *I didn't think you had it in you, Araskar.* That was her last thought. What kind of last thought is that?

A worker tilts my head to look up. The nest queen is clicking her mandibles together.

"You do not want my jelly, wide-thorax?"

"Not at all, just, uh, savoring the odor."

I go ahead and lick up some royal jelly. (Don't judge. I was putting worse than this in my body, up until a week ago. It's not bad, in a tangy, bodily-secretion sort of way. Sweet, with a hint of vinegar. Nobody tell Jaqi, or she'll want some.)

The drones step away at another particular hiss from the nest-queen. I stand up. She unfurls one of those antennae from her head and strokes my cheek.

"Will you add the best of your blood to our line?"

The way she says it, it isn't a question.

"Take the kid out," I say under my breath to Swez.

When X and Toq have been taken into the hallway, her workers swarm me and pull my clothes off.

I resort to speaking Imperial. "I'm sorry, I barely know you—"

"I am not going to take you in passion, wide-thorax," she says in Imperial standard. This whole time, we could have been speaking a language I actually know? A language with phrases that would let me turn her down. "I would, if you begged, but a girl must be forgiven for rending some flesh in the heat of passion. If you want to keep your arms, I suggest we do a simple extraction."

"Hold on now, you didn't tell me it would kill me. I could go for death that way."

"No. I think you are meant for something special, my mumbling, scarred, wide-thorax. And I need you to work this prison job. It is a good risk, one that bodes well for your seed. Hold still, and I will take what is needed."

I don't get a choice in that, as her workers pin me.

A sharp mandible emerges from between her legs, like a scorpion's tail, ending in a glistening point like a needle. "This will hurt a good bit. But it is for your cause, no?"

Of course.

She jabs it right into my left testicle.

Every muscle in my body seizes up and I vomit a little and fall down to the ground and I'm nose-to-nose with an eyeless drone's head, sweating a river from every pore, and cold as a comet, and my left nut might be going supernova.

John Starfire's voice fills my memory. "This prisoner? Inside Shadow Sun Seven? Survived a year in the heart of the Dark Zone."

"Well, wide-thorax," she says as the workers pull me up to my feet. I vomit and they lick it off the steps. "I think we have all found wisdom today."

"Or something like that," I mutter. Memory's blade just gave me a roundabout stab in the nuts.

Jaqi

THE SMOKE FROM THE boy's burning flies up into the sky, against the glowing Suits' planet. Taltus's reptilian voice booms out over the camp.

It's the Thuzerian way to give a body to fire, even planetside where you can't put too much smoke in the atmos without ruining it. The boy weren't much of a believer, but Taltus, he says the boy would sit and talk on faith with him, and was going to embrace the faith. No one has counteracted that, as none of us are preachers.

I'm staring out at the dark desert, because I can't stand to be over there.

Watching a boy's body burn, a body I should have brought back.

Taltus has been speaking in some language I don't recognize, but then he stops to translate some of what he's already said. "Oh God, highest of arbiters, foe of all darkness, Great Sun. Erdo thy servant has fallen in they service, to defend against corruption and darkness and entropy."

That en't why he died. Damn me, damn me to the Dark Zone.

"Jaqi?"

It's Kalia.

Couldn't be anyone else, huh?

She comes closer—and hugs me. She presses her face to my chest, wets my shirt with tears.

I should put an arm around her, comfort her, but can't move. I stand stiff as a corpse frozen in a vacuum, while she hugs me.

"Can we read a few verses?" She presses her well-worn Bible against my chest. Of all the things to bring in space, she brings this book, and don't no one agree about what it actually says.

"Aiya, you—you want to read some of them verses what comfort people?"

"No," Kalia says. "I want to read the verses about you. Maybe we can figure out why you couldn't, you know, do a—"

"No." I don't mean to snap at her. But damn. Now? "No, girl, I don't want to hear it." I try to make my tone softer. "En't no point."

"Jaqi, you need to learn to read the Bible, or you'll never know what you're supposed to do."

"Them prophecies are the same ones folk think might

be about John Starfire? I need to read something most folk don't agree on?"

"They're obviously about you, Jaqi. Remember when we were on the Engineer's planet—"

"Stop crazing!" I let go of her and step away. "En't me in them prophecies! I don't want to lead no religious movement. I'll get myself drunk and forget to save the galaxy!"

"It doesn't matter what you want, Jaqi. You have a duty to the galaxy, and that is something to take seriously. You need to stop the Red Peace, you need to stop John Starfire, you need to make real peace with the Dark Zone—"

"I know what I need, aiya! Need some time to think! Your books teach you how to leave someone alone?"

She tries a stern tone. "You have to learn to read."

"Will you quit ordering me around? This is why folk don't like you bluebloods!"

Soon as the words leave my mouth, I realize they are the worst things I ever said. I want to grab them out of the air before they hit her ears, and make their way to her heart and break it.

Why folk don't like bluebloods. She don't need a reminder of that. It's true folk don't like bluebloods. Folk didn't like her pater and her brother enough that they killed them.

"Kalia, I . . ."

"Don't," she snaps, real commanding, but there's a little hint of a sob about her words.

"Kalia, I . . ." Hell, what do you say when you've been that big of an ass? Burning hell, Jaqi, you went and improved on your foolishness today. "Kalia, I shouldn't have—"

"Don't talk to me!" She throws the Bible down at my feet, and runs back to the fire.

I almost go after her. I should.

But I don't. I pick up that Bible off the ground, sand clinging to its leather-worked cover. Turn the pages. Too dark to see what they say.

And if I could see it, I wouldn't understand them little markings.

And if I could understand them, they wouldn't make no sense. Folk think they make sense, but I been all over the spaceways, and religion's no different than every other drug you can get from a slimy Kurgul drone.

I en't no miracle worker. No Saint. I'm just a scab. Those words proved it. No one but the worst of spaceways scabs would say such a thing.

I leave that Bible lying there, turn around and walk out into the big black desert.

Araskar

The hoverbug zooms through the desert. Cold night air blows my hair around, cools the burn on my cheek, although it does nothing for the pain between my legs. Kurguls aren't big on painkillers.

Swez sits next to me, his hat pulled low, his wings constantly vibrating, a sign of annoyance, I think. Toq clings to X, next to me, all of us unshackled and armed on the nest queen's orders. Suddenly compatriots with these drones who were shooting at us yesterday.

Over the rumbling of the hoverbug, the rumbling of the annoyed drones all around us, and the pain still exploding out of my left testicle, I hear the faint strains of music ahead.

Jaqi's there. Good. She's safe. If . . . different.

The music's faint, and slow, like the players are drunk.

"We should announce ourselves," X says. "Drone! Give me access to the announcer on this hoverbug."

"I want to scare em," Swez answers.

"You little filthy insect, you have cost our friends enough this day, you—" I only get X to shut up when I hand her the voice-key for the speaker, that I pull from the hoverbug's dashboard.

"Don't let him rile you up," I say. "He's just mad I got some time with the nest queen."

Those wings rattle, a sign that he's challenging me.

"You wouldn't dare, asshole," I say.

"You think I am scared to go against the nest queen?" He snorts. "She will not begrudge us if we see an opportunity for more profit."

That is probably true.

X takes the voice-key and speaks, her voice booming. "This is Xeleuki-an-Thrrrrr-Xr-Zxas. We are coming home. We are safe. Do not shoot." The fire gets closer and closer on the horizon. A big fire. I suspect I know what it's for, and I wonder who the poor desert folk lost because of us.

The hoverbug roars to a stop and sets down, along with the three following us. I clamber out and hold my hands up, showing myself, X, and Toq, along with the three dozen drones behind us.

The whole camp smells of burnt meat, the smell both sweet and sour and rank, which means they're burning not just muscle, but bones and entrails. A burning body. So our newfound allies definitely killed someone today.

Taltus steps out in front of the crowd. The floodlights turn his bone mask bright white, and play off his black soulsword. "You dare return, you—" He sees me and the others, unshackled and armed.

And then Kalia bursts out of the crowd, runs for Toq and sweeps the kid up in her arms. "Toq! I was sure you were dead! Oh, thank you, God!"

"Araskar saved us!" Toq exclaims. "He made a deal and he did the slack with the nest queen!"

Everyone looks at me, halfway through my limp to Taltus.

I just smile, and try to look like I'm not limping. "You're welcome."

"You made a deal. With the nest queen." Mutters and whispers sound around the group. They all know why I came to this planet. Taltus's yellow eyes narrow behind the bone mask. He lets out a low, guttural lizard hiss, the sound muffled by the mask—

"I made a *trade*. No one's going back to the Resistance."

Taltus keeps his sword up, but nods slowly. "God be praised for your safety. And for the child's, and our sister of the Zarra." He comes forward, puts a long, scaly arm around both of the children. "You made an agreement with . . . Matakas."

"And he did the—" Toq shuts up when I glare at him.

Swez comes around from behind me. He rattles his wings, tips his hat, and offers one segmented arm, topped by two clawed fingers, to Taltus. "Coin and prosperity to us, ai, preacher? Good to be working with you."

Taltus's hand tightens on his soulsword, and, unprompted, the black blade bursts into blue flame.

"Easy now, preacher," Swez says. "Thought those swords worked on faith, not anger."

"I do have great faith," Taltus says. "It requires great faith to walk these sands, when you drones use our people as target practice, when you spread abomination across the galaxy, with your guns and your drugs, with your dirty money and your whoredoms and—"

Swez laughs. So do the other drones. "I love me a preacher."

Taltus raises his flaming sword like he's about to strike—and Kalia speaks up, thank God. "Thank you," Kalia says. "I don't care who you had to deal with, or what you had to do to keep us out of John Starfire's hands. Thank you for saving my brother."

Well, that almost brings down the pain in the left side of my boys. "You're welcome."

"Where's Jaqi?" Toq says.

"She's—" I hardly realize I'm speaking. I feel her, not far, though not in camp. Just outside camp.

The music has changed. It was, before now, a soaring, sweeping wall of song. Like all the stars' fire poured down through her, turned into music.

Worse. Not even like the players are drunk now. Slower, like something chokes off the music. Like the instruments' strings are slowly detuning.

"What's happening to her?"

Jaqi

I walk into the desert night.

Trace glows overhead. The Suit cities are bright enough that, even from the distance of this moon, yellow light flickers and glows, and the reflected light of the sun makes the planet a wide glowing crescent, dimming the stars.

I'm hungry again. I call myself ten kinds of burning fool for not eating a thing today, and curse the hole in my middle, and drink all my water long before even midnight hits. I couldn't've taken some corn before I left camp? Maybe a handful of greens just to munch on? I could've at least changed out of shorts and T-shirt. Nights get mighty cold out here, which en't a thing I'm used to considering. In the spaceways, inside the ship is warm, outside is death. But they warned me. High winds at night, cold as the day is warm. On those rare times when the moon hits the shadow of the planet and it's tipped the wrong way on the axis, the night here gets cold enough to kill.

They warned me, but I'm just a spaceways scab.

I pull the emergency blanket out of my belt pouch

where it lives. I wrap it around myself, but the wind keeps finding a way in. My feet are blocks of ice, even in their boots. I shove my fingers through the edge of the blanket and pull it close.

Finally, I find a rock to lean against, and dig my butt into the sand. The sand's freezing. This is like cuddling up to vacuum. The micro-coils in the blanket glow, faint red, putting off warmth, but damn, the wind finds its way under the blanket no matter what.

The wind dies down, as the sky turns light gray. It's real pretty. For just a minute, my eyes close, my body warming under the emergency blanket.

I'm drifting in space. It's cold, but I can breathe, like you do in dreams.

All around me, the stars. To my back, the white ribbon of the Imperial belt. The wild worlds are spread out, glittering individual stars around the wide empty patch of the Dark Zone.

In front of me, a node. But something's wrong with it. It's gone dark.

It's not a node like I know nodes. Like it en't opening to another place anymore, but just into a big nothing.

A voice, a voice made of shivers and ice, of jagged edges and ragged bloody cuts, speaks to me. *We know you.*

We watched you. We watched you, when you tore their bodies.

A voice from a mouth that has swallowed whole star systems.

I snap awake, my heart roaring, staring up at the gray sky of the moon of Trace. "Devils! Burning devils!" I jerk up, see the last of the stars in the lightening sky. And my eyes go right to the one patch of sky where there en't no stars.

"Devils en't here, Jaqi," I mumble. "Still stuck in the Dark Zone. At least for now."

Until they move on the wild worlds. Like John Starfire promised.

The blanket's warmed me, but I feel an all-new cold snaking down my spine. *We know you.* I didn't think much of it when they said it to me in the Dark Zone. Figured that was what they said to all their meals, to spook 'em.

Out here, in the freezing early morning, suddenly that starless patch in the early sky seems too close. Might it be the devils know something about me?

About the miracle?

We know you.

Something moves in the dune next to me.

I grab at my side for my gun—which is empty. Of course. I shot all my shards off at them Kurguls today, and we weren't exactly on a catch of shards before. If a Mataka found me, I'll have to hope he's a lousy shot—

No, en't a Mataka. It's a critter. A blue snakey-headed thing, slithering through the sand, with the help of two small padded feet. Its floppy yellow kill stretches behind it, leaking purple stuff.

I jump to my feet, and yell at the thing like a damn idiot. "Off! Go!" I en't never seen a wild critter but them horses. It's probably got poison and claws and spits venom from ten feet away and—

The blue, snakey thing takes one look at me, squeals and drops its meal, splits the other way, burrowing into the sand three dunes down.

I start laughing. "Jaqi, you damn fool, you faced the devil himself and you got scared of a critter."

I walk over to the prey critter it left here. Poor baby something—all floppy skin hanging off a little frame, four filmy yellow eyes staring out a bulb at the top of a tube-shaped mouth, all above a massive purple rip beneath that mouth.

It's still twitching, but I recognize them twitches at least. Seen plenty of sentient corpses. Meat in the body seizing up in death, that is.

I touch the dead thing on its head, despite my reckoning that this may not be the cleanest idea I ever had.

I don't feel a thing.

I close my eyes. The image from my dream comes to me—floating in space, reaching out to touch a node. Music, pouring out of the node.

Finding nodes and moving through them, without the benefit of codes and node-relay talkers—that's the only thing I ever been good at. What's that got to do with bringing folk back to life, and the Dark Zone, and—and music?

Music. I can almost hear it again, them sounds like real instruments and them pulses and beats like sound from the heart of a star.

The dead meat jerks under my hand.

Well shit. "Did you just—"

No, the critter's dead. En't it? Not moving.

We know you. The voice comes back to me, and I hate how cold I am of a sudden. They was waiting for me. I can't say how I know. But I know, sure as I know the feel of a node.

A distinct sound rings through the desert air. I know that. It's a horse's whinny.

Search party? The hole in my middle groans, saying it might be a fine thing to go back and have some real matter, but I ignore it—well, first I take off the blanket and wrap the dead critter in it, as I might as well try cooking the thing up, if I'm going to be out here for a while. How hard can this be?

I step into the full morning sun, into a breeze already warm and bringing sand.

And I see Z and a horse, not a hundred paces off under a tall rock, the horse grazing on what little ragged, sand-fringed grass sticks out of cracks in the rock.

As if I needed more reminders of a miracle.

"Jaqi." He's dismounted to let the horse graze. "I am sorry. You should not have seen me."

"You been following me?"

He nods yes. Like this is normal.

"You let me freeze my ass off last night, and let me sit here without a single bite—"

"At home," he interrupts, "our youth often sojourn by climbing the Great Rim, where the cliffs are so high that the great black drakk does not even dare the crags, where the wind is the icy breath of space itself. Among the high places, a soul is born. I took my own climb when I was very young. I served as a shadow, following other young people, later. I thought I might do that for you, when I saw you leave last night."

"I en't Zarra."

"You have made a kill, and seek to cook it. That is a thing to be proud of."

He's proud of the dead thing in my hand? I toss it down on the sand. "Wasn't me. Stole this off a critter what made the kill."

Z makes a scowl and a sound that I'm sure is a Zarra sigh. "There is little meat on that creature, but I can show you how to gut and skin it."

"Uh . . . okay, slab."

"Or, if your walk has finished, I have packed jerky."

"Real matter? Oh, thank all gods and goshes and Starfires." I toss the dead thing out into the sand, hoping that poor snakey-headed predator will come get its dinner back, and grab some sanitizer from Z's saddlebags to clean my hands, and then some jerky at last. "Who else come?"

"No one knows you left, Jaqi."

"So they're still back there? I reckon I walked pretty far."

"You walked in a circle. You are three miles from camp now. At your greatest extent last night, you were five miles away. If we go over those rocks"—he points to a line of ragged rocky hills, rising not far from us—"it is only two miles."

"Oh." I guess that en't much? I don't bother asking him how far three miles really is planetside. Everyone gives me a funny look when I ask things like that.

"Is your walk complete?"

I swallow jerky and water, and find the words. "I don't want to go back, Z. All that bowing. Thinking I could do miracles."

"You did do a miracle. You brought me back."

"Don't remind me! I en't got a clue how I done that."

I turn away from him—and gnaw on more jerky. "Hell, that makes it worse. I should have been able to save everyone."

"Jaqi, I—"

"Don't speak, slab. Don't tell me all about how I'm the oogie of space and the son of starlight and get me thinking all wrong. That's what got Toq taken! Got that poor kid killed, and what are we supposed to do against the whole damn Mataka nest?"

"What else is there? You cannot run."

We know you. Damn, I wish I had never remembered them words. "Don't tell me what I can do."

"Jaqi." Now this is something I en't never heard from this slab. Pleading. "What do you want me to say?"

I chew the jerky. "Just talk to me normal, Z, not like no special oogie of space. Like I'm a normal girl."

He thinks extra-frowny thoughts for a moment and then says, "I am not very good at talking to girls."

That right there makes me laugh. "Finally you said something normal."

He laughs as well. I never heard this fellow laugh. It's a good sound.

A moment later he's kissing me.

I been kissed before, but I never been swept up in arms as big as ships and kissed by a fella twice my size. Takes a minute to get my head and kiss him back, by which time he's broken off and staring at me.

"What?" I say. "That was well by, slab. Why stop?"

"I . . . I . . ."

"You trying to find a way to work blood and honor into this?"

"No," Z says. "I simply want you."

Part of me wants to tell him not to bother with a scab like me, a fool don't know what she's doing, but he starts on that kissing again and, well . . .

I en't never been one to get picky.

I pull away and gasp, "Everything works, aiya? It'll work 'twixt you and me?"

"Ah, uh . . ." Z clears his throat. "More or less."

"Good enough."

Finally this day is getting better.

-4-

Araskar

JAQI IS BARELY A MILE AWAY. And the music is still fading. I wish I could say what did it. I cannot figure what might get her to change her mind, to turn around, but—

For one second, it changes. The music roars off her, the walls of soaring strings, the rumbling deep chords in the foreground. Percussion rattles at a fast pace.

Then it fades again.

What is she doing?

Kalia walks next to me. A couple of Mataka drones walk behind us, their guns no doubt pointed at our backs, because they cannot be anything but bastards.

Kalia has told me about her last conversation with Jaqi, though I suspect she left something out. "So she must have gotten scared when I said we should read the Bible. She ran away."

"You think she doubts everything we believed about her."

"I don't know if she really believed it in the first place," Kalia says.

That could be a problem.

Jaqi seems distracted, because the music has settled to a low hum, still with those out-of-tune notes and changes in meter. Is she talking to someone? Did someone else find her first?

"I shouldn't have pushed Jaqi," Kalia says.

"It is what it is," I reply. I notice that Kalia is holding her Bible to her chest, the book dirty and ragged, sand stuck to the spine. "No use in regrets."

"It's just—I want it to be true." Her voice falls, so quiet I can barely hear. "I don't want my brother to have died for nothing. And I thought we could find my mother, with Jaqi's help."

"Your mother's alive?"

"I have no idea" She keeps her voice very composed for a scared kid. "She was visiting some of our off-world holdings when . . . the Red Peace. My father said she was safe. But then, he said we would be safe too."

I am not sure what to say to that. *I'm sorry*? There's a whole galaxy full of the dead that *I'm sorry* won't make up for.

We crest the ridge of rocks between the camp and Jaqi, and—

I freeze. The music has changed. It's definitely sped up,

although there's no mistaking that kind of beat. Rather ecstatic noises, noises that, to me, sound a bit like instruments squeaking out a legion of bent notes. I know exactly what Jaqi is doing.

"Wait," I say.

And now a low, stomping beat, under the bent notes. The kind of thing you might associate with a hot, crowded club where sentients can rent a private room for an hour. "Just wait. It should only be a few minutes."

"What are we waiting for, Araskar? Is she relieving herself? Can you tell that?"

"Yes," I say. "Yes, that is definitely it."

"We're on the nest queen's time, cross," one of the Matakas yells from behind me.

"Drink some water," I say. "Take a break. It'll just be a few minutes."

It's more than a few minutes. "She's really taking her time," Kalia remarks.

Not really, all things considered. They'll be done any second. Unless they try to go again. "Yep," I reply.

Eventually the beat tapers off, quick pulses slowing, music settling into a steady warm harmony.

I try very hard not to think of Rashiya. Even though I can feel her memories as she breathed into my ear, as she pulled me down into bed, as she ran a finger down my scars.

We start walking again, toward the source of the music. We descend the rocks, curve around a few more formations and trudge over a sand dune and I make some noise to warn Jaqi—

And we come on Jaqi and Z, both of them half dressed, him with his scale trousers half buttoned, Jaqi without pants, wearing only her shirt, and pointing warm shardblasters at us.

"Drones, you best not—wait, Araskar? You're alive!" Jaqi runs to me as if she's about to hug me, and stops herself. "And Toq? Is he here? Is he—"

"He's fine," I say. "He's sleeping. I made a deal." I motion toward the Matakas behind us.

Jaqi glares at them. "A deal with those scabs."

"Had to do something."

"How did you locate us?" Z asks.

"I, uh . . ." Oh hell, they're going to figure it out. Jaqi, at least, is going to know I got in her damned head again.

Sure enough, she nods. "Oh right, that music. What special stuff comes off me."

"Yes."

Jaqi meets my eyes, despite the fact that I'm trying to look at the ground, or the sky, or Kalia, or something else . . . and Jaqi breaks out laughing. "Aiya, slab! Reckon it had a good beat! Hope you danced!"

I think Kalia's going to say something, but she doesn't pipe up, so I speak, as awkwardly as the teenager I never was. "You coming back, ai?"

She cuts off the laughter. "I have a choice?"

"No," says one of the drones, but I hold up a hand.

"The nest queen won't care whether or not you come. You weren't part of the deal, Jaqi."

"What's this deal, slab?"

"A prison break," I say. I move closer. Speak so only she and I can hear. "There's one person in the prison who survived a year in the Dark Zone. I think they might know a thing or two about the Shir."

And to my surprise, she pipes right up. "All right. I'm in."

"You're in."

"Reckon I need to talk to someone about that Dark Zone." She takes a hefty drink of Z's water, and looks out at the desert. "Can't run no more. They're gonna find me, en't they?"

"I think we've run as far as we can."

Jaqi

"Shadow Sun Seven."

Araskar's laying out the details of his plan, and we're all

paying attention, and it might even be a nice story around a fire, if you ignore the three dozen Kurgul drones around us.

The fire we made at twilight illuminates what Araskar's drawing in the dirt for the Matakas' benefit. Toq clings to my leg. Kalia en't spoken to me yet. Reckon I can't blame her, not after what I said. I wouldn't want to speak with me either.

Araskar points to his picture in the dirt. A giant bug. He's talking about this mission, this catch in a prison, he's using to distract the Matakas. "The head, here, is formerly known as administrative headquarters for the prison. Docking control, the warden's offices, and the brain for all the mag-locks everywhere in the system."

"You can remotely disable everything from there?" Swez asks.

"Not everything," Araskar says, and those Kurguls rattle their vestigial wings. Reckon there's only one worse sound than that in all the galaxy, and that's the sound of atmos escaping your ship. "I can turn off the incinerator and then you can get in through a dispersal tube. Then someone small enough to go through the maintenance tunnels can disable individual mag-locks on the mining levels. They use Reveks to do the maintenance. The Reveks are the size of these children."

"Why not Suits?" Taltus asks.

"The Empire didn't trust the Suits, and I'm guessing the reformed prison isn't about to start."

"Mining," Swez says, and his wings rattle furiously, while his little inkblot mouth puckers up. "Really, it's cutting the hyperdense cells out of what used to be the things' lungs, and then storing them without letting them expand. Dangerous work."

"Not a place for loose shards," Araskar says. "But you can be precise, can't you?"

"Too much of a gamble here, cross. We're getting in through the incinerator? How are you going to get into the head?"

"I will take that Zarra"—Araskar points to Z—"in through the entrance. We'll pretend to be a pit fighter and his manager."

"There's a reward out for you, cross," Swez says.

Araskar shrugs. "They'll have trouble filling that reward. Lots of crosses with my face and a few scars." He points to a new burn on his cheek. "Look, you've given me new scars just since we met. Should be a great disguise."

Z breaks in. "I have heard of this place, from when I was fighting in the pits. Shadow Sun Seven runs a weekly fight, and the money is good, but the word is that the fight is run without honor."

"Well," Araskar says, "all the better to steal from them."

Araskar points at various pieces of his drawing in the sand. "Once I get in well with the other fighters and managers, I disable the incinerator. You fly up the incinerator, then once you secure the mining works, we can start moving material out. There'll be loading barges in the mining area. Have them meet up with your drop ship, lash them together, have Jaqi jump you back here through some dark nodes." The Matakas are silent, no wings rattling, so Araskar adds again, "And then put some matter in the nest queen's hand."

"Why you care about this prison?" Swez says to Araskar.

Araskar speaks to Swez, but he's got one eye on me. "There are people in there I'd like to speak with."

Swez don't bite on that, thank God and gosh. "You haven't mentioned the guards. Crosses?"

"The guards are Nbossoobissobashoolu."

Everyone looks at him all confused for a second, mostly because that en't a word you often hear from tongue and lips. "Blobs," Swez says. "You didn't tell the nest queen that."

"Fluid sentients. In an explosion, they can discorporate and come back together. Safest bet around all those hyperdense oxygen cells."

"Hm," Swez says. "We don't like this."

"You saying your people can't take on a bunch of

blobs? They don't die easy, but they're not exactly Imperial Marines."

"We cannot afford shards in that space. Not that they would work on fluid sentients. We will need to disable those guards before the mission begins. At least weaken them." Swez chews, and mutters something to his buddy. I know a bit of Kurgul, and I hear the words *nest queen rewards double-crosses too . . .*

"Aiya, scabs," I say. "Let me speak."

The Matakas turn and glare at me. They hate humanoid females, what with us being neither worker nor queen.

Everyone else seems to be glaring at me too, though. To be fair. I am their Chosen Oogie What Just Ran Off.

"I know Matakas got a vault full of disease. I know because you made all of Ecosphere 118 in Resenti sick to pull off a heist. Left a heap of bodies."

"Why are you speaking, female?" Swez snaps. "Be quiet."

"Make them blob guards sick. Just *sick,* mind you. Not killing."

"I want this female to be silenced, as she should be," Swez says to Araskar.

"Why?" Araskar says. "She's just told us what we need to do. What sort of biochemical weapons do you have in your vaults?"

Swez grumbles, and those wings rattle. "A few." He avoids looking at me and speaks, again straight to Araskar. "We may have a pathogen that can make the fluid sentients discorporate, to a degree. For a few days they will have difficulty managing their shapes. It will give certain other kinds of sentients some troubling symptoms as well. Mania, and perhaps hallucinations."

"What other sentients?"

"Mmm, a cross may have problems if he is given an enhanced dose."

Araskar nods. "I'll risk it."

"Let me call our storehouse manager. She will not be pleased to use a favorite pathogen."

I start walking toward Araskar. Swez raises his shard-blaster. "Just need a moment to talk, scab. Me and Araskar, on our lonesome."

"We're partners now," Araskar says. "You put a gun on us, the nest queen hears about it."

Swez lowers the gun. "Reflexes is all. Just a bit of free advice: never trust a female that hasn't produced any larvae."

Funny thing is, that en't nearly the worst thing I've heard off these scabs out in the dark. You should have heard what the crickets, with their three sexes, none quite like a humanoid's, used to say.

Araskar crosses the camp, and comes to stand next to

me. I smell the remnants of shards on him, burning hair, burnt skin. Smell something weird and tangy too. Makes me kind of hungry.

"So, how'd you know this about the prisoner? You pulled it out of gray girl's head?"

"That's what these swords are made for." He taps his soulsword. "When someone's taking intel to their grave, you need a way to get it. The Empire had to believe we weren't sentient to treat our memories this way." He looks like he thought of something. "You should carry the other sword. From Rash . . . from the woman I killed."

"En't touching that thing!"

"It'll let us talk without the Matakas overhearing."

Aw hell. He had to say something useful. "You reckon we'll use that?"

"You think we won't?"

I can't think of a thing to say. It all sounds mad. "By the devil and Earth that was lost, what makes you think we'll get anywhere?"

He smiles, almost a real smile, stretching out that scar in his chin. "Faith."

"Don't give me that, slab!" I stop, and I don't talk, because truth is, I'm a mess here. I want to run. I want to run so fierce it burns me up. I was made to run. I been doing it every chance I get. I even ran here.

But it won't work now.

I hate to say it, but there en't anywhere left to run to. And the whole galaxy's after me now. Oh, the reward's out for Araskar. But I looked the devil in the eye, and he knew me. I won't forget that no matter how far I run.

Like Araskar said, I got to be the chosen oogie of space. It en't true, but I got to act like it.

"All right," I say. "I'm in with whatever you think's best, slab. Still don't like you, though."

"I don't need more friends."

"Counter-resistance. Needs a better name."

"Resistance, rebellion, revolution . . ." Araskar shrugs.

"You en't allowed to pick names. I reckon . . ." Hang on, that's it. "Reckoning. We gonna make John Starfire reckon with what he done."

"The Reckoning. Day one."

He puts his hand out, and we shake on it. Two dumb crosses. Like he's reading my mind, he says, "Not what we're made for."

"Not in the least."

"Get back over here, crosses," Swez yells. "We do this, you work for me."

Well, this is a hell of a start.

-5-

Araskar

OUR SHUTTLE, only big enough for myself, Z, and X, flies out into space. Toward the node, and toward the job.

Behind us, Trace glows, even from a far distance, the lights of the Suits' infrastructure gleaming. Farther behind the planet, the moon orbits, that little scrap of desert where Rashiya's body is buried.

In front of us, a black patch blots out stars across half the sky. The Dark Zone is close here, in these wild worlds.

Between us and the vacuum beyond, where I can't see it—no one can, and only Jaqi has even the faintest sense it's there—a node.

"Take us through, Jaqi," I say into the comm. And I touch my soulsword, and I feel the resonance from the one she now wears, the one that Rashiya once had. Twenty hours.

Not so hard, slab. Talking through the swords tends to give you a headache, but as I've already got a headache from withdrawals, I haven't noticed like Jaqi has.

How's the sword feel?

Don't like wearing this sword, slab. Don't like thinking on what it's done. This is the sword killed that poor kid Quinn. Because Rashiya didn't come out of a vat, the psychic resonator in her sword, by nature, adapts to the user. It explains how Jaqi used a sword before, when she stabbed my old commander Terracor.

Watch Swez and his drones. They go off-plan for even a second, you let me know.

Aiya, slab. The Reckoning away.

The node opens up. In we go, to pure space.

For half a second, I think I might hear the beginning of music. For half a second, all the glorious things I used to get from taking the pinks—and then the node spits us out, we spin into space, and everything is silent again.

The music's gone. Jaqi gone, the music of pure space gone, and my whole body aches with its absence, my head throbbing, my testicle twisting, my burns all the more painful without her nearby.

Z's voice pulls me out of the pain. "Shadow Sun Seven. I am . . . I am impressed."

I turn my aching head and look at our objective.

From this angle, we look up, at the swell of the Threg's head and the swell of the body extending beyond it.

I've seen some big bugs in my time, but this is the biggest bug in the entire galaxy. A head the size of a decent ecosphere, a huge swollen body stretching into space beyond that, so big that you might mistake it for a moon. I can just make out, from the floodlights, the running lights of the barges, and the flare of jets and incinerators, under a mess of running lights and circuitry where there were once several swollen eyes and probiscises.

We're going to fly straight up its gullet. (Which is better than the way Jaqi'll come in, as the incinerators vent out the other side.)

"Here we go," I mutter. "Down the hatch."

Running lights increase as we get closer. Tiny ships run alongside the skin of the thing, looking for breaches, reconnecting miles of wire and ducts and checking vents, pumping a stream of extracted carbon dioxide and other gases into space. A click, and our comm automatically tunes to a transmission—advertisements. "Is the Resistance resisting trade? Is the fall of the Empire the fall of your stocks? Come to the best market in the galaxy, no questions asked, customs and tariffs only what you're willing to pay!"

I move to flip off the communicator, and Z stops my hand. He listens, and then growls, "There is money changing hands here. Far more than on Swiney. Cade should have taken me here."

"To think first of money is the way of dishonor," X says.

"That is not what I mean," Z growls.

"If I thought only of profit, I would do well here," X says.

"I do not think only of profit," Z says. "I know the meaning of honor."

"You—"

"Shut up," I snap. They've been fighting all day. I suspect it has something to do with the way Z and Jaqi disappeared into their quarters back on the drop ship, and made enough noise—and enough music—to wake a sleeping Shir.

The running lights of the prison gleam off a load of hyperdense oxygen cells, like giant irregularly shaped marbles, loaded into a nearby barge that is meeting up with its loader to go through the node.

Given that nearly everything in the galaxy either lives off an oxygen mix or has been crossed with oxygen breathers to be able to live off the mix, the stuff mined here is a mint. Reverse-cell generators, with their layers and layers of algae, can make breathable oxygen, but even the compact ones take up a lot of ship space and fuel. The only other option is to compress hyperdense cells of planetary air. One hyperdense cell, tapped slowly, is good for at least one standard mission. Much easier to store, if more volatile. But that means getting them off-planet—unless you find a creature, like a Ruuzan Threg, that both lives in vacuum and will consolidate the oxygen for you.

Three hundred years of war against Andelaxan pirates means lots of hyperdense oxygen in the bellies of these things. And lots of prisoners needed to cut it out.

I hit the comm. The screen flickers, and a bored-looking fat Kurgul drone appears.

"Customs here. You a vendor?"

"Pit fighter," Araskar says. "I sent it over in the application packet. Zaragathora. Eater of Flesh. I'm the manager."

Behind me, Z says, as if no one heard me, "I am Zaragathora. I have come to compete. Also she has come as well." He motions to X.

"Lady X," she says. "A tested fighter."

"Zaragathora." He gets the blank look that shows he's paging through computer screens. "Last competition on Swiney. You one of Cade's boys?"

"I left Cade's employ."

"Hope so! Cade's with the asteroids, word has it! Cafe Out-the-Airlock, table for one!" The Kurgul laughs and rattles his wings, a deeper thrumming sound than the little Matakas made.

Z ignores that. "This cross is my manager now. I am willing to fight in open melees, but I will reward you handsomely against seasoned competitors."

The fat Kurgul rattles his wings for so long I think he must be having a damned heart attack. "Lots of trouble there at Swiney. Lots of complication." He mutes us, talks offscreen for a while, then says, "Got someone higher-up for you to speak to."

The screen flickers, and comes up on—a Necron.

Not one of their priests, but a cross. Nothing like my short-lived pet, the NecroWasp, though, which was an ugly mix of everything dead and mean in the galaxy. This guy's a monument. He's got the skull-face, but it sits below an enormous forehead, which rises into an intricate bone crest. He wears black armor and two curved knives sit at his waist. His head scrapes a tall ceiling. Like some sort of freaky statue, commissioned by a madman.

"You're the boss?" I say. I suppose a pit fight is a decent place to worship death.

"He's the protection. I'm the boss."

I didn't even notice the guy there with the "protection"—partially because he's down at the edge of the screen. A short guy, but not just short—nondescript. The most boring features I've ever seen

Weirdly, Z and X both go totally silent.

I resist the urge to look at Z and put on my best smile, trying to look friendly despite my scars and bandages. "Nice to meet you. What can I call you?"

"My people call me the Boss. Boss Cross if you have,

heh, a sense of humor."

"Okay, Boss Cross, what's this about my best fighter being off the lists?"

"Zaragathora, Eater of Flesh. Very good record, with the right people, but one of Cade's, and delisted after Swiney Niney." He gives a very nondescript shrug and a very nondescript smile. He is somehow every minor clerk in the galaxy all at once. "You can appreciate that any business, even one such as ours, runs by a code. Any trouble with the authorities, either old or new, and . . ." He makes a hand-washing motion.

I wait on Z to say something. But he doesn't speak.

That's strange. I figured he'd pop right up and explain how much honor he's stashed, and he's the greatest fighter in the galaxy, and he's got a huge honorable . . .

But he doesn't say anything. Neither does X.

"No Resistance trouble on our end," I say.

"Your face inclines me to believe otherwise," he offers.

I try to give him a grin. "I'm retired. A war hero. Got the papers and everything, if you want to see them." I don't have anything of the sort, but given that the Resistance was terrible with paperwork, I can fake it. "Why don't we sit down over a drink and I'll give you the truth of Swiney?" I say. "Let my Zarra on the list, and let me bend your ear."

"You are free to board and enjoy yourselves. I may take

you up on that."

"Well information here. And fine fighters."

"Come aboard. Enjoy yourself. We may talk."

And then we're back to that fat Kurgul again, explaining our clearance to land.

That's not much, but it'll get us on board. We'll have to figure it from there. I turn to Z and X. "You could help me do some of the talking next time."

"It is him," Z whispers. "Ancestors truly have looked on this mission."

"I recognize him as well," X says. "He must die by our hand."

"You know this Boss Cross?"

"We called him the Faceless Butcher," X says. "He murdered a million Zarra, a generation ago, when the Empire's mines expanded."

"The entirety of clan Karras-rrr-Seriya," X says. "The Empire gave them a commandment to leave their ancestral land, and they would not. The next day all were gone. Strong men, mighty women, but children and elders as well. Their land poisoned, their people a memory. The galaxy turned a blind eye."

"It is well known among our people," Z says, "that the Faceless Butcher uses a complex psychic resonator so that he will not be recognized. It is attuned to pure-space transmission frequencies. In person or on comm, you will not recall his appearance."

"That's . . ." I was going to say that was crazy, but I realize that I have no recollection of what Boss Cross looked like. He was just . . . boring.

"The psychic resonator is also designed to damage recordings and pictures, but a few unaffected pictures survive. We study them. Every pore. The shape of the nostril, the cowardly slope of the forehead." Z is speaking now like he's reciting something. "Our elders show us those pictures, and each young Zarra memorized every feature of the Faceless Butcher, memorize the words he said when he murdered our relatives. I vow that before we leave Shadow Sun Seven, he will be dead for his crimes."

"That's not really . . ." I start to say.

"I too vow," X says. "I will stand with you, Zarag-a-Trrrro-Rr-Zxz."

"It's great you're on full-name terms, but—"

"Then together we shall shed his blood, Xeleuki-an-Thrrrrr-Xr-Zxas."

"We must. Let us vow by blood." She whips out a knife.

"Yes, our blood now will seal this—"

"No, it won't!" I stand up and snap. "That is not the damned mission. This is a quick extraction. Our job is to get the virus into the air, turn off the incinerator, and get out!"

"You do not give me orders, Araskar Cross," Z says. "You are a soldier, and you know nothing of honor in killing—"

"I know plenty about killing. More important, I know about keeping a mission going, and you are a soldier under my command now."

"I am no *soldier*." Z makes it sound like a dirty word.

I don't move. "You know where this Faceless Butcher is now; you can come back later and get him. I've done a lot more extraction missions, and killed a hell of a lot more people than you, and you'll take orders whether you're a soldier or not."

"What?" Z's frown gets even more chiseled and angry. "You have not. I have surely killed more in combat than you."

"Endanger this mission, you endanger Jaqi and the children." I turn around and start piloting the ship toward the bug's mouth.

"You do not command us on the matter of our personal honor, Araskar Cross," X says.

"Final goddamn word!"

Z bends down, and speaks right into my ear, damn him. "I am not a soldier. I am a warrior. A warrior is commanded by honor's demands." And after a minute, "I am sure I have killed more than you in combat."

I really don't like Zarra.

I pilot us in to Shadow Sun Seven.

———————

Jaqi

<u>You get through okay?</u> I grip the sword by my side. Feels funny, wearing a sword, for all that I was made to do so.

No answer from Araskar.

Oh, yeah, he told me them swords can't talk through a node-relay. Hell. They ought to be able to.

I let go of the hilt. It en't like I'm in a hurry to talk to him. I miss Z. Wouldn't mind talking to him. Or getting him alone. But even Araskar would be better than this. Kalia and Taltus have found something worse than bowing.

It's Bible study.

"It's the wording here, in the Genesis of the Empire," Taltus says, pointing to something in that Bible. "He is a cleaver, a weaver, a gatherer of souls, who unites and divides."

"That doesn't talk about how she brought Z back from the dead, though," Kalia says.

"Hey," I say, "anyone seen any good holos lately?" They look up from their books. "You all seen them Scurv Silvershot holos? Bill watched them every night. Finest shot in the galaxy." They all look up and blink. "You seen the one where Scurv and Ariel Singh rob the memories from the big automaton, the thing what's in the center of the galaxy and they remember every single thing ever happened but they can only remember it if they keep off the whiskey, and they can't?"

Kalia doesn't answer. She hasn't spoken to me directly, about anything but scripture, since we left the planet's surface.

"I haven't seen it, but you just told me the whole story," Toq says.

"Do not speak that name," Taltus says. "The real Scurv Silvershot is a wicked murderer, who killed Saint Valir. No one should lionize such a criminal."

Well, en't that a way to kill the conversation. I grab a set of coveralls and say, real loud, "I'm going to take a look at the controls. Seemed a little touchy before."

"Jaqi," Kalia says, "Wait. I have an important question."

This is about the first thing she said to me since I blew up at her. "Go on."

Taltus speaks. "Jaqi, sss, when you brought Z back, sss, did you have the sense of crossing a great gulf?"

When I don't answer, Kalia adds, "Like you were reaching out? Or calling him back?"

"Why you ask me about that?"

"We're trying to figure out what the scriptures say about you," Kalia says, "so we can figure out—"

"Kalia," I say. "I—look, I'm mighty sorry, I just en't in no mood for Bible time."

She nods.

"I'm mighty sorry."

She don't answer me.

"Go look at the ship, sss," Taltus says. "You will study with us later, yes?"

I finally get to leave. Hell, I've been in some stinky recycled-air rustriders, but this one has a thicker atmos than I ever tasted.

I pass by my room, which Z and I were in not three hours ago. A much happier time, that. The room stinks. Sign of a good party.

Course, it all went spacewise once Z started talking about the miracle, in his own way, and what he figures I am.

———————

Z and I lie on the floor, slick with sweat and totally starkers. The plates that hold our last meal lie next to us. Were the table not bolted to the floor, it would have had some trouble, too.

"You learn this in them pit fights?"

He turns, pulls me close with those big old arms. "I did not learn how to make love. The knowledge lives in my bones. We are the oldest people in the universe. We taught lovemaking to the stars, and they burn still because of it."

I slap his bare hind and he grunts like I don't get how serious he is. "I need some water, slab. You best let me go. Less you're ready to go again."

"It would be unmanly to try and feast again so soon, when the belly is so full."

Who talks like that?

I drink some water from the bottle we took off the moon of Trace. Last of the good planetside water. Recycled piss after this, though a girl couldn't be choosy especially after she had the workout I just did. I reckon them Zarra crossed with humans or Jorians at some point, because while we didn't fit together exactly, everything worked.

"I ought to ask you a question," I say, going back to the floor to sit aside him.

"I will answer what I can, by honor."

"You and this pit fight? You worried?"

"It is what I can do for the mission. Araskar's plan is wise. The Matakas give us resources, and we speak with this prisoner who is so important to John Starfire."

"It's another pit fight! Last one had that Necro-Thing what did you in!"

He bares his teeth. "That creature was … filth. If I must die in blood and honor, I shall, and it will be for the good of this. The Reckoning."

"Can't believe I came up with such a name." I run a hand along the muscle of his shoulders, trace the tattoos. "You en't got to be in such a hurry to get killed, Z. You got a future."

"You agreed! Araskar's plan is wise!"

"It's an evil good plan, but we don't need you in no pit! Taltus could hold himself fine in a pit, and he knows the spaceways 'round con men. You need to watch your life, now it's been given back." He starts to speak, but I stick my hand out to shut him up. "You ought to have little ones, what you can pass your stories to."

"Children? Jaqi, we cannot have children, not without using a vat."

"En't got to be me. We got X right here. I been thinking of, uh, inviting her in." He goes quiet. "I en't picky, you know! She's a nice slab her own self."

I joked before that Z only has three facial expressions. I think I just found the fourth.

It's somewhere between smelling something weird and a little sad.

Did I say something wrong? I figured he'd be ready

and rutting to be with another Zarra, 'specially if I'm rutting for her too. "En't a thing, I'm just talking about trying the girl out. Have a party. See where it goes."

"Jaqi, my people mate for life."

Hell, what now?

"To one person."

"Hang it now, I didn't sign up for no—"

"It is done now. We do not—share."

I stand up, looking down at his big old self. "I en't one—uh—not to be shared." *Aw, hell, Jaqi, why don't you ask these things afore you jump to it?*

He stands up, his horns clattering against the ceiling, hunching over me—then sits down again. "What did you think this was?"

"A bit of fun! I didn't sign up for no life sentence!" I grab my clothes and pull them over my sweaty skin. It takes a hell of a lot longer than I would like, so I'm still getting them on when he speaks. "You know me well enough to know I don't take a tumble as no wedding vow."

"It is my people's way. Our lives are short, and so often wasted."

"Wasted how? You reckon this is waste—"

"Wasted by drugs. By alcohol. By foolish resistance to Imperial forces."

"And what's better than—"

Z holds a hand up. "I wasted myself in the fighting pits, looking for petty honor. But your cause is just. The ancestors met me at the River of Stars, and when you called, your call was so powerful they chose to send me back. I have watched my people waste themselves for petty vengeance or anger. This matters. I must be one with you now, Jaqi."

"Oh hell. Don't go there." He moves to pull me close to his naked self, but I put a hand out and stop him. "Just . . . just come out of them pits alive, now." I sigh. "I like you, Z. I en't ready to get spousal, though!"

"I am sorry." Didn't expect that. "I . . . I did not think to tell you. As far as I am concerned, it is decided."

"No it's not, fella. We'll talk it over when you get back." I want to hug him, but I'm also real fired up at him. "Give me this, then. Promise you'll stay well enough to come back and work this out."

"I will promise that."

I hope he's listening to Araskar. Seems to me those are two fellas meant to get into trouble together.

6

Araskar

ON THE INSIDE, SHADOW Sun Seven is all new money laid over rot.

New, shining bulkheads, in warm blue plasticene, have been place against walls that were previously just bug-mouth. They flash advertisements for various things available, apparently, in the lower levels—*Stall 17-B: The Best Fried Curliqs in Space! Stall 183-ZZ: Come See the Qurruq Dancers, Worth Traveling to the End of the Floor!* The place stinks. It's the kind of stink you notice right away, but everyone must be used to—the stink of the Ruuzan Threg's slow decay, the meat left on its exoskeleton that still hasn't been entirely cleaned out. Smells like bad food, booze, every kind of rutting known to sentience, the burn of holoshow bulbs, and that everpresent stink of the rotting insect.

"We must go with you to see the Butcher," Z says, as we bounce along in zero.

"Absolutely not."

We pass inside the field, suddenly held firmly to the floor by Imperial Standard Gravitational Force. It feels good. None of the art-grav itch. Brand new, Keil Quality field of the highest degree. Holds your feet to the floor and lets you walk with a nice pressure on the bones.

"When will you see the Butcher?"

There's a few stalls set up for those waiting on customs. I use a little bit of the Matakas' cash to get a chunk of Routalais chocolate. It'll make a nice present for the kids—if Jaqi lets them see it. The bluebloods probably had it after every meal growing up, but she'll go mad for this stuff. You taste subtle shades of rich chocolate in everything for days.

"Why do you buy that?" Z asks. "We cannot waste time!"

"Don't tell me; sweets aren't honorable?"

At customs, another fat Kurgul drone—by the tattoo, one of the Hukas nest that Swez loves to hate—is taking weapons. Z pulls his belt knife, as does X, and they put them in the box. I take my large soulsword and set it in, and, under his eye, the small one too.

"Here's your tag; redeem it when you leave."

Damn. How am I supposed to keep in touch with Jaqi? I look over at Z. "I thought these places let you keep a sidearm of some kind," I say.

"This is unusual," Z says, "but we are sitting on miles of hypercompressed oxygen; I imagine a loose shard can be death."

"Soulsword's no danger for that."

"You don't like it, you can turn right around," the fat Kurgul says. "Out the airlock."

"No," Z says. His eyes catch mine, and say what we're both thinking. *With everything else going on, we'll have to find a way to steal these back too.*

We step through the gate, and I say, "So, no plan."

"Let us see what we hear in the bar," Z says.

"I could use a drink."

"Drinking is not an honorable use of our time. But I suppose it is what *soldiers* do."

Not going to hit him, not going to hit him . . .

We sit in the bar and watch the fight, me nursing a beer and Z and X nursing water. We're not watching the actual fight—the windows that look into the fighting pit are adorned with betting bars, loaded with sentients trying their money on the fight. Instead, we see highlights, constantly running on the holo feeds above us, their projectors hanging from endoskeletal struts that once helped to keep this bug together.

This was all the creature's throat once. After that it was exercise yards, and other facilities for the benefit of the prisoners. The on-site hospital has been turned into gaming rooms and fighting pits, and treatment centers for the fighters. The cafeterias are restaurants, where the tourist can refuel, then go back to betting on pit fights.

The prisoners are housed below, in a block of cells built into the oxygen mines. I imagine life has gotten a lot worse for the prisoners, without those facilities. And I can imagine that, with the market collapse that followed the Resistance's takeover of the Imperial Exchange, Boss Cross really doesn't care what happens to the prisoners, as long as they get money.

I look back at the pit fight. A heavily armored bipedal sentient is clambering through a rather nice-looking stand of fake trees, while Slinkers wait for him on the other side.

"We had to clear a nest of those things out of our camp on the moons of Keil." I point at the Slinkers on the screen. Slinkers are terrible, man-sized segmented black things that are mostly made up of a stinging tail, except for four spindly legs, each one ending in a claw they can hook to keep their prey in place while they sting it. They sing when they've enclosed their prey—a weird, shriek-ing, twisting song. "My slug Helthizor called them 'wankers.' Whenever they would sing to scare us, the whole camp would yell, 'Quit wanking!'"

Z and X just give me another frown. Perhaps this is the Didn't Know Araskar Had Friends frown.

"Don't worry, they're all dead," I mutter.

X takes a dutiful drink of her large cup of water. "How will you sneak in to see him? The Faceless Butcher is cunning. All know this."

"Diplomacy."

They're still staring at me incredulously—at least I think that's incredulous. Incredulous frown or just Irritated Frown or just Regular Frown We Woke Up With?

"Let me try this. And don't move," I say to the Zarra.

Just as I get up, the grubby Szz comes around again. "Drink up, friend!" he gurgles. "Come on now. Drink a pink."

I stop, and for half a second break out into a fresh sweat. "What did you say?"

"Drink a pink with this one. Have a brain bullet with your booze. Come on now." He waves the drink at me. "Dissolved right in there. Good for hours."

Sweating. All over. My body is hot, blazing—no, I'm cold, about to shiver, like I'm naked and about to feel the touch of a lover. I know the smell, woven through the alcoholic sweet smell of this drink.

A drink and I would't have to think about Rashiya dying, wouldn't have to remember anything, wouldn't have to think about Jaqi and Z judging me for what I've done . . . A drink and the music would come back. I wouldn't have to wait for Jaqi.

"Araskar?" X puts a hand on my arm. "Are you disturbed?"

I'm still staring at the drink.

"I will not sit here being dishonored while you freeze up!" Z snarls at me.

That gets me moving at last, and the Szz's hairy snout swivels from me to Z, confused, until Z says, "Peddle your poison elsewhere, filth!" and that gets him moving as well.

Barely been two weeks since I sent my pinks out the airlock with the ashes of my poor troops, killed in action by Jaqi. Only been a few days since I last sat and melted into the music of the universe. My body twinges, little flutters and beats up and down my arms, in anticipation of the first pill melting on the tongue.

No. Not ever again.

Why do those words sound so weak?

The central surveillance area, where the warden's office once was and where the boss now resides, is a long pillar going through the immense tunnel that was the monster's throat. The central eye of a prison—everything would have centered around this one artificial pillar, which, I'm guessing, connects up to a similar central control area in the mines.

And there's a blob, near the closest entrance into the command structure.

A bulbous blue tendril comes up and it gurgles something into the translator. "You wait outside like anyone else," the robot voice says over the gurgles.

"Boss wants me here," I say. I shouldn't be this shaky when trying to make a deal. "We spoke earlier. Information about what went down on Swiney."

"Doubt it," the blob gurgles. "Go on."

"No, try him. Come on now." I should make an offer. I pull a few Imperial bills from my pocket.

The blob eyes the cash in my hand. "What's that for?"

"For lots of things," I say. "Could be for a favor now."

Something shatters loudly behind me. I turn around and stare, along with the guard, at a very changed holo.

Some dumb drunk has managed to fall into the pit. The holo shows him, an awkward Zu-Path, looking stupidly around. The holo then switches to show two Slinkers, backing off the prey they were hunting, and the whole room fills with their eerie song, that screeching, high warble like the wind.

"How the hell did that happen?" I ask the guard. "You bought the best creatures money could get but lousy plasticene?"

The blob just stands there.

"Aren't you going to do something?"

He gurgles something that sounds foul, but translates only as "Those stings will kill me too." The translator attached to the top of his body crackles and he says, through the translator, "Patron is at fault. Charged the glass to see if it would hold him."

"The glass *doesn't* hold the patrons?"

A Slinker pounces, and the poor drunk scatters away, screaming, but he doesn't see two more climbing up the fake rock behind him.

The armored pit fighter won't save him; he's moving slow and stupid, as if the Slinkers got through his armor.

The Slinkers' singing fills the air, high shrieking as they surround the poor Zu-Path. Twisting, warped song.

I turn to go to the pit. No one's going to help this poor idiot, and I've seen enough innocent idiots die. At least I know how to kill Slinkers; keep moving so it confuses their sense of pressure, and make sure to cut off the stingers.

And then the whole crowd of drunks roars, as the ones gathered around the hole are shoved aside and two figures appear in the pit.

Two tattooed figures.

Of course.

Z and X now stand in the center of the rocks and sand of the pit. The Slinkers' song increases and their tails sway toward the Zarra. One Slinker is still chasing the poor drunk. Z runs up behind it, grabs the Slinker around the tail, right below the poisonous barb. He actually swings the thing around, its tail spluttering and bubbling with poison, and tosses it toward a nearby rock. An audible *crack* rings out.

The crowd roars.

X, also bare-handed, faces off with a Slinker more interested in her than the drunk now. It lashes out with its tail, and she dodges, strikes again, and she dodges, and she actually smiles.

I didn't know Zarra *could* smile.

X dances backward, and picks up a rock, and when the Slinker dances closer, singing all the while, she lobs the rock with perfect accuracy and hits it in the head. It strikes, but now it strikes blindly. She must have gotten its eyes.

Z picks up the poor drunk Zu-Path and slings him overhead, up through the broken window. Then Z turns, and just avoids another Slinker's tail.

All the Slinkers are circling them now, hungry shrieks filling the air.

The heavily armored fellow staggers through the rocks near Z and X. Falling from the poison, he holds up his spear to X.

She shakes her head no, turning down the spear.

And smiles again.

Damn it, at this rate I'll pull them out of there in pieces—

No. Another Slinker lunges, and strikes at Z, and not

only does he dodge it, he seizes its tail and this time, lifting the entire monster overhead, he snaps the tail clean off.

And he roars, a high, ululating cry that drowns out all the Slinkers' screeching song, and lashes out with the severed tail, Slinker viscera flying everywhere.

X hurtles more rocks, knocking the creatures off the rocks. One sneaks up behind her, and she sees it, and actually moves too close for it to strike with the tail, right in its face. It rears up and tries to sink the hooked claws into her, but she grabs them, pulls it off-balance, and digs the heel of her boot into its eyes

The blob guards finally drop into the fighting pit just as the Slinkers are moving away from the Zarra. The blobs fire stun-bolts from the micro-shards in the shock sticks to drive the monsters back.

Z and X are covered in blood and guts.

And smiles.

Well, now I know what it takes to get a Zarra to smile.

The blobs lead them, and the dying, heavily armored sentient out of the pit. People shout all over the floor, roaring and toasting the two Zarra with drinks aloft, and I hear, "When are they fighting again?" and more importantly, "Who's the manager?"

I shove my way through the crowd over to Z and X, who are being carried to the bar, and have ordered a couple of very light ciders to celebrate this impromptu victory. I hear Z over the crowd. "It was not an honorable contest," he keeps saying, and X adds, "You will see us in an honorable contest, soon enough."

"Not bad," I say to Z, once I've managed to shove aside a few hangers-on. "I hate to say it, but that will probably get us in to see the Boss better than my plan."

"That was no plan," Z says. "We saw a contest without honor, and it was honorable to intervene, if only for that fool's sake."

"It wasn't planned."

"Of course not."

Of course burning hellfire in my balls not.

The blob I was speaking to reappears, grumbling constantly as he shoves through the crowd. The translator buzzes—it seems to be having trouble with what he's saying.

"You the Zarra's manager? The cross with the scars?"

"That's me." I give my best ridiculous smile.

"The boss will see you now."

7

Jaqi

YOU KNOW HOW I ran to the cockpit to get away from folk?

Swez is in the cockpit.

I really am not loving this job.

I try to ignore him as I open my flaps of tools and crawl under the control panel. He rattles his wings and chews some noodles with his little puckered mouth, using his face-tentacles to spoon the noodles in, and watches me from under that damn hat.

That's why the damn shuttle is so touchy. They rigged up a skim-box, kind of thing that you stick on a thruster switch to make it burn extra hot, and are running all the switches for piloting this thing through it. Idiots. "You flying through a hollowed-out asteroid?" I mutter. "You racing in a planet-slug's guts? No one needs the controls this touchy. Nest queen en't impressed by stupid."

"This Reckoning business," Swez says. "What's this about?"

This is the first time this scab done talked to me directly. I stop fiddling with the controls I been trying to fix—"fix" being my preferred word for removing all nonsense.

"Female."

"Drone."

"The boys say this is all part of a big plan. You figure on taking down John Starfire." Swez pulls the edge of his hat down, to cover his tentacles.

"That's right." I pick up my wrench and go back to wrenching their nonsense apart.

Swez chuckles. "What've you got against the savior of the whole galaxy? The fella who freed your own kind?"

"He tried to kill the children."

Don't surprise me that Swez chuckles again. "You humanoids get so invested in your offspring. You can always make more. I've blown whole lairs of larvae and pupae up if it was for the good of the nest. You ought to just save the ones that might matter, let the rest die."

I reckon I must have done something real awful to have to work with these Matakas. Would be nice if all them gods and goshes would tell me why I need to get punished.

Might be worth learning to read the Bible, if that's in there.

"Why does Starfire want them kids, anyway?"

"Got his reasons," I say.

"You think you've got something better to replace him, girl?"

I slide out from under the control panel, just so's I can glare. "Anyone could replace him! *Drone,* he's selling the whole galaxy out to the devils!"

"Eh. That's what every politician says about someone they dislike."

"John Starfire made a deal with the devil. Peace with the devils means giving them more to eat. You're a damned fool but you en't stupid."

"Everyone knows he made peace. Peace with the Shir don't matter much to your average citizen, selling jewelry to pay bills on some shit ecosphere. They're thinking about the bluebloods' tariffs, the bluebloods' pride. Thinking about how the humans finally got what's coming, no longer able to control the cash flow of the galaxy. I seen you with that blueblood girl. You think things will be the same for you once you're back in your place, she back in hers?"

"Shut up, scab."

"That girl thinks of you as a bodyguard. A servant. Just like all servants, just need a little breaking in."

I ignore him and pull the components of the skim-box hard as I can.

"Here's what sentients care about, girl: their wallets.

Everything else comes after a warm oxygenated room to sleep in. They don't care if a despot or a moron rules them. They care about trade. You're a smuggler—I shouldn't have to give you this talk I give to new drones. Hell, can't believe I'm giving such talk to a female, anyway. You're all hopeless. Can't understand ethics."

"Why don't you go flap them noisemaking wings out the airlock, then?"

"Aiya, don't curse me. I'm no fan of the Resistance. They might as well have vented all their cash into space, for what they did to the markets. So maybe I'm taking a little interest in you, enough to give you precious advice." He leans over, smelling like cheap synthesized thurkuk. "Ditch the bluebloods, or buy a nice little maid suit."

I spit right in his little black eye. "Never."

I expect him to grab the wrench and whack me. Instead he actually laughs, and them damn wings rattle away. "That's no way for a servant to talk! You'll get broken in soon enough, I reckon."

———————

Araskar

"Do you want to clean up first?" I ask Z. I don't know why. I know what the answer is going to be.

"Of course not. This viscera is the honor of battle. If you cannot even smell the honor in the viscera that coats us, then I truly despair of your senses. Soldier."

One of the blobs buzzes us into the Faceless Butcher's central pillar. "The Boss," gurgles the blob's translator. "He's got ways to keep misbehavior down. Just so you know."

We are left standing in one antechamber, waiting for a second set of doors to open.

Z and X exchange glances and X says, "We will not kill him at this moment. We await the proper time."

"Stay focused on the mission."

The door buzzes open and reveal the NecroSentry. It must reach ten feet to the ceiling. It holds a tall spear, topped with a sharpened bone head. It leers down at us, and with foul breath like rotten meat, it groans, "Death."

"Ignore him. Terrible company." Boss Cross appears from behind the NecroSentry, and extends a pallid little hand. I take his hand. It's soft and puffy and warm as a dead animal. "His personality's absolutely dead, heh."

"Oh."

"Come in, come in. The Zarra of Swiney Niney and

their manager, heh. Love the Zarra." The Faceless Butcher wrinkles his nose. "The zany, ah, let us say *zestful* Zarra."

"I changed my mind," I whisper to Z. "You can kill him now."

"Now is not the proper time," Z replies.

"I know, I know, it was a . . . never mind."

He pours some clear water from a pitcher and drinks it. I've never noticed that someone can drink in an especially boring way, but there really is nothing special about the way he drinks. He smacks his lips. "Doesn't taste great," he says. "Distilled from the moisture in the oxygen cells, so it tastes like the moisture of three-hundred-years-gone sentients. Don't be scared by an old teetotaler, heh. I take one drink and go right off. Can I get you any cider? From Routalais orchards in never-terraformed soil."

"Something strong," I say. Everything hurts, from my testicle to my head, my dry mouth wants the pinks, and if I'm going to be in withdrawals from hard drugs, I will damn well drink.

"Would the zealous Zarra care for some?" He holds up the water.

"No," Z snarls, like this is an insult.

"They're not thirsty. They drank, ah, some blood." I'm not at my best with this headache.

"That was a brave, possibly foolish thing you did out there," Boss Cross says. "You fought on Swiney? One of Cade's boys?"

"I did." Z looks over at X. "She did not."

"What he means to say," I add, "is that Swiney was a heap of trouble. For everyone." Boss Cross leans in. "Cade got himself killed, and no one was quite sure how, and there was a heap of pit fighters left without a manager."

"And the Resistance was involved. Is that how you connected with these . . ." He stops, holds up a hand monitor, and scrolls through a list of words. "Zoophagous Zarra?"

"Zoophagous?"

"It means carnivorous." A nondescript grin. "I love words. Don't you? Such a myriad of meaning."

I try to sound like Jaqi. Like I belong among space scabs. "Aiya. I decided a while back I'd had enough of the Resistance. Enough of 'consolidation' and fighting when the fighting was supposed to be over."

I sound too bitter. And the drink is too strong. Better rein it in.

"Mmm, yes," Boss Cross says. "The disgruntled soldier. I see."

I give a deliberate look around the room. "I would love to see how this place works when you're ready. Never seen an old-style oxygen works, breaking apart the hyperdense cells."

"And I'd love to give you a tour," Boss Cross says. "Pride and joy, the oxygen works. Come along."

"Now?" I say. "Before they clean up?"

"They are fine," Boss Cross says. "Just fine. They wouldn't be the first pit fighters to come see me in, heh, their natural state."

The NecroSentry grunts "Death" as if this is relevant.

They lead us toward a central pillar, running through their round room. The doors slide open, revealing a lift with a complicated, thumbprint-coded set of controls.

This will be the first step. I get the pathogen into the air supply. After that, I'll have to figure out how to get up one more level, to the controls for the incinerator.

The lift begins to descend.

"This was prison yard when I first came here as the warden," Boss Cross says. We pass through the various fighting pits. They have been set up to resemble different ecospheres—one is the sand and rocks of a desert, while another is dotted with plasticene reconstructions of trees, and the running water of a creek, and another still is the spindly catwalks of an orbital space station. Holos play in the background, adding to the sense of realism, holos that create a feeling of distance and space.

Z, no doubt despite himself, gasps. "A magnificent place to fight."

"We used the holos to try and create a serene feeling for the inmates, when that mattered. Since the Empire fell, I had to find a creative way to make the prison self-sustaining. It is a tricky, heh, thing. I've been working on a replication of Zarra-kr-Zar itself. Lovely world. Spent some time there years ago. Cannot forget it."

"Yes," Z says. "Zarra does not easily forget—that is, it is not easily forgotten."

The elevator continues down, and the doors open to a swampy atmosphere, instantly humid and moist and choking. Green mist fills the air. We step out into the roar of the oxygen works. It's a dark room, lit mostly by running lights along giant pillars that march away into the distance, the lights obscured by the green mist.

The place stinks like every sentient in the galaxy got together and farted.

"Watch your step." The floor is rubbery plasticene that is supposed to help us keep our grip, but it's so saturated with thick beads of moisture that we nearly slip. Over the roar of the oxygen works, the Boss stammers, "Hyperdense cells are great for ships that don't have a good system in place, but using them on this scale was tricky. This is the only part of Shadow Sun Seven that's not part of the bug's body—it's a kind of 'collar,' and if we have any problems, this is where the mines will separate from the, ah, head. A protection measure against prison revolts, you know. Any instability here—any explosion—and tourists are safe, don't even need to look up, backups will kick in until we can reconnect."

"If there is a problem, and the oxygen works stop, what happens to the miners? The prisoners?"

He just shrugs, and points around him, changing the subject. "Ignore the green stuff—can't help bleeding off some of the original bodily gases trapped with the air in the first place." He leads us across the floor, all of us, even Z and X, testing the ground carefully, trying to maintain our balance as we get closer to whatever final destination he's got in mind.

I eyeball the nearest pillar, while holding my hand over my nose. The pillars contain the centrifuges that process the cells. Every few moments a loud *bang* echoes through the chamber, and the beads of moisture rush across the floor, sucked to the small grates at the bottom of the pillars.

Boss Cross points to the nearest pillar. "The hyper-dense cells are sucked up into the centrifuge and get spun until they lose integrity. Lets off the residual gases."

Luck already. I must have done something right today. "Where do the cells come from?" I say, trying to maintain conversation while I slip the Matakas' tiny vial out of my pocket. It's dark and hazy enough in here that I don't think either the Boss or the big NecroSentry lug notices what I'm doing.

"There are hoppers under the floors, running on conveyer belts. Workers fill them up and other than that, the whole system runs on automation."

We start to walk, and I pretend to slip, falling over. Z reaches down to catch me, but not before I crush the vial against the floor, right next to one of the grates.

A moment later, the grate sucks the contents of the vial right up, into the centrifuge, and from there into the air-processing unit.

There. That's done.

I stand up, and say, "Sorry! Slippery floor!"

As soon as I stand up, there's someone else with us. Standing right next to me. "Hi," Rashiya says.

"Uh, hi?" I look at Z, who is looking at me oddly. "Hello?" he answers.

"I'm just here for you," she says. "Just call for me. It's not bad over here, you know. Not bad at all, being dead. Much better than the alternative."

Oh, shit. I remember now what the Matakas said about this pathogen. *Some hallucinations for humanoid sentients.*

Rashiya smiles at me. "You'll like being dead."

Couldn't it have been rainbow-colored space slugs?

"You just missed me too much," she says.

I hate how my mouth moves against my will, mutters, "I did."

Memory's blade gets another stab.

8

Araskar

BOSS CROSS PRESSES HIS hand against the door, and we step into what must be one of the loading chambers, although no one's in here at the moment. It's cold, not cold like vacuum, but cold like refrigeration. The wall is piled with hyperdense oxygen cells. They shimmer, piles and piles of varied orbs and egg shapes, shining with the thick skin membranes that help keep the oxygen contained. They stretch up the wall, in a pile. The cold probably helps the cells retain integrity.

Z and X both look up.

"You should look up too, Araskar," Rashiya's ghost says.

I look up, and there's a dead body hanging from the ceiling.

A Zarra, even bigger than Z, immense and broad with tattoos standing out against his ice-white body, where it's not bloody and beaten. Massive meat hooks jut from his thighs. Black blood has dried everywhere, in a scabby stalactite hanging off his head.

He's dead.

"It's cold in here," the Boss says, his voice now flat, without any trace of mirth. "Good for preserving dead meat."

"What is this abomination?" Z roars.

"This is only the latest one." The NecroSentry slides the door shut, and I become very aware that the three of us are stuck in here with a lot of volatile material, the Boss, and the NecroSentry. "There's always Zarra coming here. I wanted to have a little talk with you two. See, the first kind of Zarra, they fight, they take their pay, and they leave, if they make it through the ring. Those are the ones with sense. The second kind, though, always seem to feel the need to come after me. If that's your goal, well, we may have to call you the zygomorphic Zarra, for I will cut you in half."

"You've been saving that one," I say.

The NecroSentry grabs Z by the back of the neck and shoves him down to the ground. X he does not touch, but the Boss pulls out a soulsword and points it at X. "Come near me, and you'll deal with one of these."

"We didn't come here to kill you!" I shout.

"I want to hear it zoom from the Zarra mouth," the Boss says. "I believe you took an opportunity on Swiney. Plenty of people licked up the scraps on the floor there, heh, and I believe you are a bit, heh, scrappy."

"Oh, God," I say.

"Of course we came here to kill you!" Z says.

What the hell? What is he doing?

Z tries to stand, but the NecroSentry forces him down—nonetheless, he grits his teeth and squats, pushing up against the bony hand shoving him down. "I have sworn vengeance for my people and I have memorized your featureless face. This is the moment for which I have always waited." Z bares his teeth. "I will fight with—" The NecroSentry cuffs him, a blow so hard it chips one of Z's horns.

The Boss actually laughs. Backlit by the running lights in the floor, reflecting on the stack of hyperdense cells, the little nondescript face could almost be scary. "Shame for you." He points to me.

"But this is not how it is supposed to happen!" Z says. Almost whining.

"Is he lying?" Rashiya's ghost says.

I think so. As close as he ever comes to acting.

"Tell me how it's supposed to happen, and no zigzagging, Zarra," the Boss says.

"I would fight each of your foolish fighters, and then I would challenge you, before all the station. Honor demands you fight me." The NecroSentry cuffs him again, and this time he leaves a welt under Z's eye, but it doesn't seem to bother him.

"You really think I would fight you in front of the whole station?" The Boss laughs.

"Honor demands it!" Z snarls. "You must!"

"Why would you not?" X adds. "They are your people, and you owe it to them to defend your honor."

The Boss continues to giggle. "Tell me more about this fight we're going to have."

"When we have won glorious battles, and more honor than any Zarra in history, we will fight each other, and the winner will gain the privilege of killing you."

The NecroSentry actually allows Z to stand up.

"Sometimes I forget how much I love Zarra," Boss Cross says. "Not a zero for my love of the Zarra. You won't try anything until we're in the, ah, fighting pit together."

"Of course," Z says. "Do you think I have no honor?"

The NecroSentry actually grunts something other than "Death." "You believe this?" it asks the Boss.

"I believe that Zarra will always do the honorable thing, no matter how stupid." The Boss looks straight at Z when he says it. "I'm tempted to let you live, just to see what you do."

"You must let me live. I have sworn to defeat you." The way Z says it, it's a basic fact. *You must clean this dish, because it's dirty.*

"Huh," Rashiya's ghost says. "Nothing like appealing

to someone's prejudice to sell your case."

I stand and look between the Boss and Z.

The Boss ponders, and then finally he chuckes. "Why not? We'll start your fights tomorrow," the Boss says. "You can finally wash. I was worried I'd have to kill you without you washing."

"Blood and honor to us all," Z says. "I look forward to meeting you in the ring."

The Boss just smiles, and says, like it's normal, "But just to make sure you don't try anything, your manager will stay with me. In a cell of my choosing."

Hell.

Well, I've still got an incinerator to shut down. The cell will probably be closer to the station's brain.

Rashiya starts to speak and I hold up a hand, and then realize that as far as anyone else can see, I'm holding a hand up to the dead man hanging from the ceiling, as if he were about to say something.

Same difference. I talk most with the dead.

I force myself to look past Rashiya at the Boss, the Faceless Butcher. "I'll be fine."

9

Jaqi

I TAKE THE TOOLS back to the shuttle bay, having done what I could with the controls, though I think they've hot-rodded this drop ship so damn many ways I could work on it for years.

Here in the bay, the Kurguls are still playing their favorite game of stick-the-drone-with-the-shard-stick. They all cackle when their latest victim screams.

They also don't see Toq, who, I reckon, snuck away from that dead dull discussion about the scriptures to get some food. He's rifling through protein packs, on the wall of the hanger bay, not far from the circle of Kurguls. I walk over and put a hand on his shoulder and he freezes.

"Hungry?" I say. I keep one eye on the yelling, cackling Kurguls.

"Kalia says we can't have anything till dinner. She's so bossy."

"No arguing there." I sigh and grab a few of the chocolate-flavored ones, which taste more like bulkheads than chocolate. I should have asked Araskar to grab me some of that Routalais chocolate, the stuff that a sentient won't stop tasting for three days. Had it once and had the best three days of my life, aiya.

On the floor of the cargo bay, the subject of their game screams again. And then, before I can shield Toq's eyes, before I can react to even show I'm here, the Kurguls, all the drones, as if by some kind of signal, grab the poor fellow's arms and tear them off. They dig into his carapace and rip off the vestigial wings. They thrust the hot poker into the poor guy's eyes. And only when he's had his tentacles ripped off and shoved down his little black mouth, only then do they notice me, staring in horror at the casual way they've just killed another sentient.

"Female," one says when he sees me staring. "What do you need here?"

"What the burning Dark?" I say. "You just killed a fella! In front of a kid!"

"You have no business here, female," another one says.

I turn Toq around and cover his eyes. "En't you got no sense?"

"There are many drones, and few queens. This is not a thing you should worry about, girl. Go back and wait on word from the cross."

Toq shakes in my arm.

I can't help it—in a move that reminds me a bit of

Araskar, I put my hand on the soulsword at my waist. "You don't do that business on this ship! Not with children around! You forget who led you to this catch?"

"Girl, you are little trouble to us. You may have your cult, but a shard has put a quick end to many a cult. Stay out of our business."

They all break into cackles at that.

Toq clutches my hand. "Why'd they do that?" He's staring, horrified, but he's seen enough in the last few weeks that this en't quite moving him to tears.

I lean down to him. "Listen up, boy. There's scabs, and there's folk. Them there—they en't nothing but scabs. They'll kill anyone, they don't care a whit, to get a thing they want. Them Vanguard were the same sort. You and I—we're folk. We want other folk to live their lives, to live right." I can't help thinking of what Swez said. *Folk just want to take their check and live.*

Well, it en't true of everyone.

"I get it, Jaqi," Toq says. "I know." He leans into me, for a little hug, and I take him in one.

"Which one is Araskar?"

"What?"

"Is he a scab, or a folk?"

Araskar. I think of how angry I was with him, thinking about how he could have stopped this all back at Bill's. But then, he saved us, and he found about the only person in the galaxy who might understand my miracle, perhaps—in the heart of a prison, but still someone who knows the Dark Zone. "He's—he's folk now. Weren't before."

"How come you yelled at him? Kalia says he can see into your mind."

Oh, kids. Crazing kids. Crazing, talk-way-too-damn-much kids. "Let's go back to Kalia and Taltus."

"Okay," Toq says. "If Araskar's folk, we might need to rescue him."

"He'll take care, fella. You just stick with your part of the plan."

-10-

Araskar

I'VE GOT ONE HOUR until Jaqi comes through the node. I don't have my swords. Last night, I slept maybe fifteen minutes in my repurposed cell. It wasn't just the NecroSentry grunting outside that kept me awake. Had it managed to go three minutes without "Death," I would still have had a ghost pacing the room.

She stands near me now. "Long night? Haven't seen my pater sleep in years. You'll get used to it."

I ignore her. She's not real.

"Not real, but you're glad I'm with you, aren't you?"

Yes, I do. That's the saddest part.

"Look at how useful I was. You pulled all that information from my head."

"Memory's blade, remember?" I mutter.

"How could I forget?"

Now, we're sitting in Boss Cross's private viewing booth, about to watch Z and X join the fights. "That's mixed for crosses, it is," Boss Cross says, pointing to the drink. "Don't be scared, heh. If I meant you harm, I'd be armed, heh heh."

"Oh, hell," I mutter.

"He's just trying to lighten you up. God knows I tried," Rashiya says.

He gets to his seat, flips on the display, and the latest fight comes on the holo. "About three times the booze that I'd give any other sentient. Added some raw thurkuk secretion—that's the stuff would get the devil itself boozed."

I mime drinking, let it touch my lips. "Thank you."

"There's your Zarra, right as red. Right as Red Peace. Ha!"

On the holo, Z moves into the ring, and roars. He's wearing only a loincloth, hands and feet bare, and he's got one weapon, a short spear that won't work well against the shield of his enemy, a huge green elephantine Rorg. Its long snout twitches, armed with a special flail.

This level is mostly rock, but it'll fool you—it has a number of traps, false places in the ground, which means both Z and his opponent are moving slowly. Geysers erupt randomly, bathing them in steam, but the top-of-the-line cameras keep the focus.

The Rorg moves in closer, lashing out with its nose-flail. Z backs up in a circle, and then, with crazing speed, he bolts in, catches a blow on his spear, knocks it aside and kicks out at the Rorg's feet. Z's attacked a couple of hooks to his boot. They shred the green flesh of those elephantine, stumpy legs. The holoshow gives us a loving look at the shredded green hamstring.

But then he trips. One of the holes in the ground catches Z, pulls him down. He takes a blow on the arm, stumbles up, backs away, going easy on the foot that fell through, hopping away in an undignified way, rubbing at the dark blood on his arm.

"Tell me, then, my fellow cross," Boss Cross says. "How exactly did you get hooked up with the zippy Zarra?"

"Told you. Jumped ship at Swiney."

"I did some poking around, heh, as I do like a game of poker. Swiney was a full Vanguard division. You have rank?"

"Not now."

"Good. I had rank once. Rank stinks. Stink is rank, heh, get it?"

Okay, now I take an *actual* drink. A big one. Kills some of the headache, although my testicle is hurting again.

How to get out of here? The NecroSentry is waiting just one chamber over, and Boss Cross is holding a shock stick at his waist. One hour.

One damn hour.

"You do stupid things when you're drunk," Rashiya's ghost says.

"I could use some stupid right now," I mutter.

Boss Cross talks again. "Your whole division was lost a few days later, I found through, ah, privileged information. Precious, principled privilege. So you got out just in time."

We're interrupted by a loud grunt from the NecroSentry. He looms over us and growls, "Sixty blobs called in this morning! Sixty!"

"The lab find anything?"

"Death," the NecroSentry says.

"The blobs are going to die?" Boss Cross's voice actually has a hint of emotion, and he casts a suspicious, if unremarkable, eye at me.

"All will come to death." Under Boss Cross's stare, the NecroSentry says, "But this may not bring them to Our Necrotic Lord yet. A very mild version of the Rurica. We have reports of hallucinations and fights on the—" The NecroSentry taps a comm on its head. Although it's got no visible ears, it still mutters, "What?" into the comm. "Another one?"

"Go," Boss Cross says, casting one wary eye at me. "Be back in three minutes."

The NecroSentry just gives a growl.

"Short-handed?" I say.

"A little flu for the Nboo. Tell me more about yourself. A few more drinks."

"You know it all," I say.

He waits. It seems he's convinced he doesn't know it all.

"So, you've got this whole prison at your command? Fine assignment for a warden."

"Oh, everything's automated, but yes, brain of the prison's right through there." Boss Cross nods, points to a nondescript black door along the wall. "Climb up there, you'll be in the original brainpan of the beast, and the brain of the prison."

That confirms Rashiya's briefing. A maintenance entrance to the control chambers from the upper levels.

Down below, Z leaps in close enough that he can grab the Rorg's serpentine nose, and chop it off with his spear, despite the flail that beats at his arms. Covered in equal amounts of Zarra and Rorg blood, Z whips the bloody nose into his opponent's eyes, then kicks the Rorg backward—right into one of the pits, big enough to swallow him up. A geyser fountains up and the Rorg screams as he's burned.

Z stands over the Rorg while the wounded sentient woozily pulls his bloody self out of the hole, stands before Z, and roars.

Then Z delivers a stabbing blow his opponent can't catch on the shield in time.

"Ooh! Now that's a kill!" Boss Cross lets out a belly

laugh that sounds as forced as everything else about him. "That right there will take him far!"

He pushes a button and a Zuurian attendee appears near us, bearing a platter.

Oh, shit.

On the platter, vacuum-sealed in a little container, is a package of the pinks.

"Ever had one?" he asks me, as he breaks his open. "No better way to forget the war. Take these, you might almost believe the Chosen One when he says us crosses were made for marvelous things."

Shit.

"Together?" I say.

"Told you I'm an old teetotaller," Boss Cross says.

He must have scanned me. Must be able to tell I'm hurting for these. Or maybe he knows more than he's saying about me. Maybe he's talked to John Starfire. Maybe the whole damn thing is a trap, and maybe, just maybe, Jaqi will figure it out and not come through—

Now I'm crazing.

I know what Araskar, the responsible soldier of the Reckoning, should do. Use the drugs as a distraction, to get into the nerve center of the prison and disable the incinerator and the mag-locks on the maintenance tunnels that will allow Jaqi and the kids to get in. The NecroSentry still isn't back.

But, you see, Araskar, the out-the-airlock fool, who couldn't save his friends or find a way out of this crazing situation, could take these. He could forget, for a second, Rashiya with his sword in her chest, asking him not to take her memories.

"You might even get me to shut up," her ghost says.

Could just forget, for just a moment, forget the war again, instead of always having to come up with another clever plan, another way around death, when he doesn't even want to live.

I take a handful and drop them into my mouth.

And I almost swallow.

My mouth is wet and my skin is saturated in sweat and I can taste the damn things turning to ooze on my tongue and I want to swallow but I thrust them to the side, to my cheek. I take another handful.

"Well, then." Boss Cross stands up, and brandishes a shock stick. "Now that you're relaxed, why don't you tell me why the Resistance is so interested in a cross with your scars, and why your soulswords ran up a—"

Then I jump on him, shove the handful of pinks down his gullet with one hand. With my other hand I seize his left hand, push the shock stick down.

I keep his mouth closed. His slobber washes over my hand, but I keep him gagged. He groans and tries to talk but I keep a tight grip, shove his jaw closed. He bites his own tongue and blood drips between his lips. That jaw stays glued.

He's stronger than he should be, fighting me with the shock stick, trying to raise it. I shove it back, grab his wrist and push down, until the shock stick connects with his own body. He jerks, lurches against my grip before he manages to turn it off.

The pinks in my own mouth are turning to ooze.

I have to spit them out, or in a few minutes, I'll be high and it'll be anyone's guess whether he or me will look a bigger idiot. I certainly won't be able to keep this grip.

I have to spit them out.

Not swallow them.

A faint stirring swirls at the edge of my mind, the headache leaking away into rising strings, Rashiya's death vanishing into sweeping whorls of music.

"Actually, when you're high, it'll seem like I'm really alive," Rashiya's ghost says. "Imagine the fun we could have."

Damn it all to hell and the Dark.

I spit them out onto his shirt.

He keeps fighting me, for an admirably long time until the enormous amount of pinks I jammed down his throat takes effect and he struggles less and less, Boss Cross's body going into the limp, stupid mode that I remember so well.

The elevator rumbles. NecroSentry coming back. Probably a personal assault alarm on Boss Cross's body. I have maybe three seconds. And I'm on fire with the need for drugs.

"Admirable," Rashiya's ghost says. "Don't you want to at least take some of that for later?" She points to the mess on Boss Cross's shirt. "Or kill him?"

"Killing him," I mutter, hating how my body is screaming for the drug, hating myself for giving it up, "would attract a lot more attention than making him look like a sloppy drug-addled fool." I drag him over to the door, scan his wide-open, vacant-staring retinae.

The maintenance door opens.

Up I go.

The maintenance route to the nerve center is a tight tunnel, winding up through metal and meat both, mostly around neural links as thick as my arms. I hear Reveks, chattering in the distance, but luckily I don't meet any.

I reach an entry area before the nerve center. Rashiya knew all the access codes for this place; I enter a series of five codes, hoping they haven't changed the codes since she got her intel.

The field vanishes.

"You're welcome," her ghost says.

I go to the bug's brain.

It's dim in here, lit mostly by the screens, and light

coming through windows that look down into the pit. Reveks man the works, little ratlike things hunched over the controls. Nerve tissue pulses overhead, sending electrical flashes through the room. They've wired much of the machinery, in a strange Imperial parallel to the Suits, into the original nervous tissue of the Threg. I suppose if the electrical system is there, you should use it.

Lucky for me, the stink of old insect meat and the chemicals they use to preserve it is strong here. And the lack of security is keeping them too busy to smell me.

"Someone messed with the fuses on thirteen! Got a whole network down there!"

"Look at that—this fellow's just trying to snatch a hyperdense cell. Where's the blobs?"

"Door just opened. Boss being evil nosy?"

One of them flips on the camera in Boss Cross's office, showing him in a state of stupefaction. I take a minute to thank the Starfire that they were distracted while I shoved pinks down his throat. "Aiya, look at this!"

"Thought I smelled pinks."

"En't like the boss—aiya, look at that! Blackout at customs! Where are the blobs?"

"All sick, aiya!"

"Someone gonna rob us blind, them blobs don't get better!"

Rashiya speaks in my ear. "You remember the

schematic? You got it right out of my head."

I do remember, thanks.

I crawl in the dark, under desks to an empty station. The Revek who manned it has gotten up to run down a few levels and fix another problem.

Incinerator. I page through a few sets of schematics. Incinerator.

There it is. Right where I though it would be. It works off a normal sub-routine; all I have to do is disable it and they won't notice until it starts to get a bit backed up and they have to reboot, by which time Jaqi will have done the work she needs to do, and the Matakas will be well into the mines, stealing barges full of oxygen.

Not just the incinerator, though. The prisoner's in 2416; I also disable the auto-record feed along that hallway, so that once we're gone, the Resistance won't be able to pull up pictures of Jaqi and the others.

Work's done here. Ten minutes to spare. Look at me, accomplishing a mission for once.

"Boss doesn't get high. Something's funny here." Two Reveks chirp their way along next to me. Overhead, the nerve tissue pulses, and I press myself as small as I can under the desk. "Smell anything?"

"Can never smell a thing in here. But . . . yeah, I smell them pinks. You think someone's double-dipping?"

Hell, I should have disguised my smell. Should have

rolled in anti-oxitate or . . .

"You double-dipping?" They chatter in some Revek patois I don't quite get for a moment, and then the first voice says, "You best share! I get tired of this evil smelly place too, aiya!"

"Got weed, not pinks."

"Aiya, now I heard they go real fine together. You sure?"

The other Revek chatters something that sounds a lot like exasperation. "I share, you tell me what the Boss wanted with that catch, aiya?" another one asks.

"En't no catch," he chirps. "Just a couple of soulswords from customs. Boss wanted to check the frequency and serial number on the resonator, to see who it was issued to."

Frequency and the serial number on the resonator, to see who it was issued to. Except, supposedly, those kinds of records have been destroyed. Soulsword registries passed through one of the central financial databases on Irithessa. In theory, the registries were all destroyed by the Resistance. But that's only if John Starfire has even stopped production of new crosses in the vats.

If he hasn't, we'll never beat him.

Those vats could produce ten thousand troops a day, ready for war within a week.

And if Boss Cross did what I suspect he was smart

enough to do and reached out, John Starfire now knows I'm on Shadow Sun Seven.

Also, I'm stuck hiding under a desk, with no clue how I'll get out. And ten minutes to go until I have to talk to Jaqi through the swords a few feet, and a million miles, away.

I wouldn't have had to deal with any of this if I had got high.

Jaqi

IT FEELS RIGHT, TO be sitting in a cockpit again. Feels right to have my hands on thruster control, coming up close on a node that'll take us to a job. I en't used to working for myself, after all. En't too bad to have a place to go, a job to do, a catch to make. Even in a stimmed-out little Kurgul rustrider.

"Any day now, cross," Swez says.

"We just hit the twenty-hour mark," I say. "Take it easy, drone. I'll get us there." I reach out to the node and—

Music.

Normally, taking hold of a node is just a thing I do. Like pissing or stretching after a long sit in the captain's chair. This time it's different. I hear that music, running through all of me. Like it's rain falling into my ears and hitching a ride through my bloodstream, notes meeting each other and merging together down in my guts. Pouring up out through my eyeballs. Like light through a scrap of worn fabric.

And we're through the node.

"That way, female," Swez says. I barely hear him. I can't quite put a feeling to this. I feel like I touched something of the miracle there. Like I found what you might call God, or the Starfire.

"Female!"

I blink, look around the cockpit. "Jaqi?" Taltus asks. He puts a hand on my shoulder. "Are you all right?"

I force myself to look down at the controls for the drop ship. "That music," I say, mostly to myself. "Why now?" Why a node?

I blink and see Shadow Sun Seven on the viewscreen: a big huge bug looming in space, about as big as ten ecospheres and some small moons.

"Take us in, female! Stop wasting time!"

I don't answer Swez, as he don't deserve it. I pilot us toward the incinerator in the bunghole of this big old bug.

We're jamming everything we can, using the Kurguls' own home-grown system. Turns out that one reason they're such good smugglers is that they can use the same frequencies they speak to their nest queen on to jam Imperial communication.

The things you learn in the wild worlds.

The ship lurches one way and another as I try to compensate for the usual problems with trajectory coming out of pure space. Makes it harder that my whole body feels like I just got the slack-shakes, or maybe had a fine cocktail. That music made me feel mighty strange.

Were there words to it?

"Female, are you paying attention?" Swez snarls.

"Yes! And this damn thing is still touchy," I mutter. They must have hooked up another skim-box I didn't fix. I breathe on this stick and it takes a hard left.

I fly with the traffic, as the main port cut into the bug en't far from the incinerators. And quite a bug it is. Never seen a thing quite like this. The front of the thing is all lights and ships swarming, and then the back is a massive swollen belly and carapace, stretching into space. Thing could swallow up Swiney Niney about fifteen times. Bigger than most asteroid mines. The skin is made up of these thick scales, hard like plasticene, reflecting the running lights of the oxygen barges and the drop shops and maintenance craft that run along it. It's so big I figure we will hardly be noticed, which is a fine thing, but I en't so sure I can find the incinerator without Araskar's help.

So this is it. This is where we take our first step in our Reckoning. Up a bug's hole.

Jaqi.

There he is, right on cue, like a fist whacking the inside of my skull. Slab, you there?

You can get in. Incinerator tunnel 14-ZC. And then, a moment later, I may be in trouble.

<u>Araskar?</u> Nothing. <u>Araskar?</u>

"Correct, female!" Swez growls behind me. "At this speed you'll crash into the side of the station!"

"Hang on, drone," I say. "Just trying to keep your blood pumping."

"Are you worried about those maintenance ships?" Taltus says.

"Unless they see us go in, en't no difference. Shady place like this, there's lots of ships in the neighborhood. Usually dumping cargo."

"Dumping cargo?" Kalia asks. "What do you mean?"

"Well," I say, "if we was, in the old times, running a load of guns that was too hot even to take in port at an evil scabby spot like this, we'd stick out an anchor—a set of smart thrusters on a net, see—and leave the catch out in the dark. Thrusters are programmed to stay within a certain vicinity, so barring a comet or another ship, you're solid."

"Oh," Kalia says. "That's interesting."

"Best to go far," Swez says, pulling that hat down again. "I prided myself on finding a dumped catch, in the days when I worked the spaceways. A good sonic bounce will pick up everything you need."

Oh, I should have figured that, with everything else wrong with them Kurguls, he was a catch-grabber.

"Pilot us in, female."

"Working on it, drone." I reckon Swez and I have reached an understanding, and that understanding is that he annoys the hell out of me.

I guide us down, a few miles under Shadow Sun Seven. I may be all turned around by miracles and Bibles, and hungry—again—but I can pilot.

Here's the trick. I set the drop ship pointing "up." From here, I can just see, with the naked eye, flares of the incinerators.

"The incinerators are still working," Kalia says, nervousness showing through.

"Just one tunnel he disabled," I say. "Place like this has at least a few dozen trash tunnels. You get better flames if you put a set of six medium-sized tunnels down, instead of one big hind-hole tunnel. Don't you worry. We'll be in and do our part and be out." And we'll meet a scab who lived through a year in the Dark Zone, and knows what's going on in the mind of the devil.

Only thing I can read is distance charts, and I reckon I got this charted well. We're a good mile out, and once thrusters fire to put us on course for the tunnel, I need to turn everything off so we don't blip no long-range. Thrusters have got to fire right. Just right, to bring us in at the angle we need.

I run the numbers a few times, and looked at the charts, and I find the tunnel Araskar done talked about, this 14-ZC, and I figure that a three-second burn would be good on any other drop ship with any other thrusters, but just to be safe with this touchy thing, we ought to give it a two-second burn.

Burn. Thrusters fire. I shut off everything in the ship.

As the lights shift off and the reverse-cells grind to a halt, Swez says, "Minimal talking." We en't got a ton of at-mosphere, and it's got to last until we get up inside the prison's oxygen.

Up we go, toward the bug's hind-hole.

We pass in and out of the paths of a few floodlights; it won't matter much until we get a lot closer. Then we best hope the ash and frozen clouds around the incinera-tor hide us from any naked eyes peeping the sensors.

It's hard to, by sight alone, figure on which one of them vents we're going into, as the vents are discharging smoke and ash and bits of half-burned matter, freezing the minute it hits the hard vacuum.

Everyone winces as bits of frozen matter ping off our hull. It's thrice-sealed synthsteel, made to take a shard hit, and no debris should punch a hole in it, no matter how fast it was ejected, but still, en't a good feeling to hear things pinging off your hull, when they should be getting et by the sense-field.

We barrel up through the mess. Smoke. Ice. Little bits of other trash.

"Wish I could see," I mutter.

And for a second, I get my wish. For a second, the chunks of rapidly freezing matter part, showing one tunnel not flashing with fire like the others—and we are not on course. Way we're going, we'll leave half the ship on the left rim of that tunnel.

"Shit, turn it all back on!" I flip the switches, and Swez snarls, "What are you doing, female?" but I en't got time—I need a little bit of controlled thruster burn—and I get it, and I fire the thrusters to put us back on course, but we're going in a lot faster now—and there's the open end of the incinerator, and I have to use thrusters to correct, to push us right up, into the smoky tunnel.

The ship groans and screams. It's hit Shadow Sun Seven's gravity now, the artificial gravity field used to push material down these tubes, and we lurch fit to give the bends. My stomach turns around ten times. I hear one of the kids puke. Thankful to my cross genes I don't do that.

The thruster burn carries us on, damnably fast, too fast. Our ship catches the wall of the incinerator tube and *screeches,* the kind of long, groaning scream that you know en't doing any favors for anything in this ship. An injector jet, what would normally be shooting flame, flies off the tunnel, crashes against our windshield, rocks the ship. I fire thrusters again, trying to stay in the center of the tunnel.

"You shouldn't have anything turned on!" Swez yells.

"Shoulda coulda!"

The other Matakas are yelling too. And the kids. And Taltus, I reckon, is praying. Lots of noise. Our ship lurches again, and damned if that don't feel like a blown thruster, now jerking us around whether I want it or not.

"Jaqi, we need to power down, sss," Taltus says, all calm-like. "They'll have seen us on the long-range by now, but they will consider it only a blip if we power off."

"How we going to brake?" We may be pushing against an artificial gravity well, but we still entered this tunnel going too fast.

"We'll have to trust the gravity to stop us."

"We can't—" I stop that. En't no other option, not when I don't know if our forward thrusters are working. I pull the power and everything shuts off—and we go careening up the tunnel, still going too fast for that artificial gravity to slow us down. Careening up and up and—

I hear something. Some door up there's opening. Now this en't great either—

A cascade of fleshy bits comes down the tube, and smacks into our ship with a loud wet *slop*.

The ship groans and shivers, and the metal screeches

with the stress, and we come to a halt, held in an evil blanket of meat.

"What the hell is that?"

"That, I suspect, is the by-product of cutting hyperdense oxygen from miles and miles of lung tissue, sss," Taltus says. "It is leftover muscle and lung tissue, bloated with water and chemicals used to break it down. God puts interesting challenges in our way."

"Delicious."

"Well, it's slowed us down." En't done the ship any favors, but we come to a stop. Now we're packed in a tight layer of pink squishy bits. "Time to get out and swim."

Swez growls at my back, and the hum of a shard-blaster prepping fills the cockpit. "Swim fast, female cross."

Araskar

You wouldn't think I could be this patient. Maybe it's the drugs.

"It's not the drugs. You're more patient than you think. You waited me out, after all. Fooled me, pretended to be on my side while you were planning to kill me." Rashiya's ghost sits, tapping her fingers idly on the control panels in this dimly lit room.

I wait under the desk until both Reveks get up, and I reach over and grab my soulswords, long and short, at last.

And the music rushes through, the sense of Jaqi so close I could almost touch it.

<u>Jaqi. You can get in. Incinerator tunnel 14-ZC.</u> I add, though I'm not sure whether it'll matter, <u>I may be in trouble.</u>

I attach the swords' sheaths to my belt, with the same precise moves I practiced for years in the Resistance.

Now, how to get out?

"Well," Rashiya's ghost says, "we're inside the thing's actual brainpan, which means there's going to be a wall of tissue and plasticene between us and the exoskeleton. Which means, if you cut through a wall, without cutting through any connections, you should be able to find some area I can crawl through."

I slice through the nearest bit of untouched meat, what seems to be just a cell wall. I can't cut much, but through my sword, I feel the resistance of a layer of plasticene along with the brain matter.

I squeeze through the hole.

It's immediately colder in here—and I recognize the heavy material above me as the inside of the Threg's exoskeleton. This is good. I crawl out and around layers of preserved flesh and plasticene together, around the enormous nerve clusters now being used to run the Imperial system here. I'm just between the structure within the bug and its skin.

It takes a while to find my way back, but I manage to stay out of sight behind a platoon of Reveks crawling along the cell walls a hundred feet down, and follow them through more tunnels.

I set off a couple of alarms, but without the blobs, no one comes rushing.

When I make it back to the gambling floor, that same scuzzy little Szz is holding drinks up. "Well, look who was too good for a pink yesterday!"

"What?"

He points.

I touch my chin. Bits of pink dust come away. My first impulse is to lick them off my hands. No.

"You think you're so good, but today you're high as five suns! Heh, heh, why not have more, then? Drink a pink from a poor peddler."

"Why not?" Rashiya's ghost asks me.

"No!" I say. "Look, where would I find the fighters? I'm a manager."

He doesn't answer that, but his eye stalks point at my soulswords. "You en't supposed to have them swords."

I lean over and whisper, "You see any guards around here?"

Those eye stalks twist around, scanning the whole floor. The blue spheres that were so everpresent on the gambling floor yesterday are nowhere.

"Show me to the fighters' locker room."

Smart little scab. He does so.

There's one blob at the door to this place. I stop, wait, afraid of what this blob might do, but he only gurgles something that sounds profoundly uncomfortable, and a large mass of blue mucus slides off him to spatter on the floor. The translator doesn't even try with that.

"Ah, I'm the manager, remember?" I wave, trying to keep my soulswords hidden.

The blob buzzes me in.

Yes. This is working. This is going to work. I walk in to the smell of steam, coming from what must be the locker room showers. I'll just grab Z and X, and with any luck, there'll be few enough guards that we can get back to our ship and go and meet Jaqi and the others, and—

Z steps out from the steam, totally unmarred, and entirely naked.

"You healed fast," I say. Not a scratch on him. Not a burn, or a bandage, or the signs of synthskin gel-packs.

What's more, on his leg, where the geysers burned him, his tattoos are faded. Like new skin's grown over them.

"Wait a minute," I say. "How *did* you heal so fast?"

"The ancestors bless me," he says.

Whatever Jaqi did to him, it seems to have lasting effects. "Grab some raggy and let's get the hell out of here. Boss Cross is out, but the NecroSentry will know I did it. Come on."

Z nods. "One moment."

He returns with pants on, and X comes with him, looking much the worse the wear for her fights—she's got several still-gelled patches of synthskin on her shoulder and arm, and a bandage around her leg, pants now cut off at the knee.

"What did you say of the Faceless Butcher?" X asks.

"I force-fed him drugs," I say. "He'll be out cold for a bit, but that NecroSentry will know it was me. Pathogen's working, though. Hardly a blob to be seen out there. We'll get to our ship and—"

They have stopped walking, and are standing there in the hallway. Z is fumbling at a locker.

"What are you doing? What could you possibly have in there?"

"Weapons," Z says. "To help us."

"We're fine! We don't need weapons! Let's go!"

Z opens the locker, and tucks something into his hand, the details of which I cannot quite see.

"Let's go!"

Z walks up to me. "This troubles me, Araskar. We carry our victories to the ancestors at the River of Stars. Today, both Xeleuki-an-Thrrrrr-Xr-Zxas and I carry much honor. But we would lose all that honor, and be in greater debt, if we left the Faceless Butcher alive." He sighs. "You truly could not kill him?"

"Z, the mission," I say. "Think of what Jaqi would want."

"It is honorable to kill John Starfire, Araskar," X says. "But more honor is gained for our people if we kill the Faceless Butcher. I was once like you, Araskar. I joined the Resistance. I learned the purpose of the Red Peace. I lost my honor, fighting for dishonorable causes."

I want to slap their stupid tattooed faces. "Look, there's a lot more honor in taking down John Starfire than—"

Z interrupts. "Our ancestors would disagree. You have no ancestors, so I will seek to explain it. Though John Starfire curses the whole galaxy, the Faceless Butcher has offended our people in particular. I know you do not understand honor, but you understand degrees of vengeance, surely?" He holds his hands up at different levels, like he's giving a lesson to children. "Here is the wrong John Starfire has done. While it is great, it affects us less. Here is the wrong the Faceless Butcher is done. These are called the degrees of vengeance, and the ancestors—"

I am so very very sick of Zarra. "There's no goddamn ancestors waiting to carry you anywhere! They're all dead, like we will be too in a moment! You're the only person in the entire damn galaxy that ever came back from the big Dark, Z, don't you go wasting it. Follow the mission!"

Z wants to rip my arms off, I can tell. But he settles for words. "Do not mock my honor, soldier. How many innocents have you killed?" He leans forward, horns down. "You had best hope that the ancestors do not greet you at the River of Stars, for they will carry the cries of those innocents you murdered."

Rashiya's ghost stands next to him, to remind me of all the dead. "You want to shut your mouth," I snap.

"You *soldier.*" Z spits on me. "Follow your orders, and what have they gotten you?"

It would be stupid to hit him.

Araskar the responsible soldier of the Reckoning, the smart one who saves lives and survives battles, wouldn't hit Z. Araskar the responsible soldier needs to reason with them, get them to remember their commitment to Jaqi and to . . .

Araskar the out-the-airlock idiot has a hell of a headache, and just spit out his first hit in weeks. And this guy's an asshole.

I punch Z in the chest.

Ow.

My hand crumples, and I think for a moment that I might not be able to hold a soulsword for a while, and the pain shooting up my hand is almost enough to drown out the pain from my head.

Z's eyes go red, and his cheeks blow in and out, and then he picks me up, throws me head-first at the wall. I roll off the wall. Jump back on my feet, and duck his blow, but I'm too dizzy, and he's fast—I can't avoid getting caught by him in a crushing wrestling grip, but I punch his ribs over and over with my one free hand, doing little good—

X grunts from behind me.

A sudden rush of pain, followed by a cooling sensation like cold water, washes over me.

Z lets go of me and I can't stand up. I flop over like a drunk.

"They gave us drugs to help ease the pain of battle," he says. "Taking them would be dishonorable, so they should suit you. We will put you in a place where you will be safe, until our task is done. Then we will escape this place."

I can't move a muscle as they pick me up and shove me in the locker, then close the door.

I'm finally high. High as five suns and it doesn't even feel good.

-12-

Jaqi

"JAQI!"

"Yeah?" I say back to Kalia, through the comm in my helmet. This is the first time she's talked to me about anything save religion since Trace.

"This is"—she's talking in bursts—"the grossest"—big pause—"thing in all space!"

Although there's atmos pumped into this tunnel—helps the burn—we are talking between helmet radios, given as we're swimming up through the sea of lung-meat, a sea of pink fleshy flaps.

"Yep. En't many scabs can boast of what we done. We went right up the bug's butt, and now we're swimming through its guts."

Toq giggles. "We're in its butt-guts!"

"Evil big butt-guts, that's right."

"Ew! Ew!"

Thick pockets of the tissue honeycombed with holes like the tunnels out of an ecosphere; splatters of rotten, cut-out bits cascading down every time we make a hole to climb up. Normally the incinerators would be blasting away, burning these bits as they fall in.

Above us, Taltus's soulsword burns bright blue as he carves his way through the mess. "We have reached the bottom of some kind of funnel now," he says. "It is widening, sss, on a slope. I will attempt something."

Taltus fires a harpoon. A *pop,* audible even in here, a flash and more bits rain down, cut apart by the shard in the tip of his harpoon, and Taltus hands down a line to Kalia, who hands it down to me. "I think I have gained purchase on something above this incinerator with the harpoon," Taltus says. "Hang on to the line."

"Swez, you hear me?" I speak into the radio. Them Kurgul scabs are still back in the ship.

"I hear you, female cross."

"Oh, I done stepped up from just *female,* drone? Aiya, scab, you know how to treat a girl! You keep this up, we'll go all the way to 'female cross with the hair.'"

"Do not waste my time, female."

I know I shouldn't worry at a Mataka, but damn is it fun. "Might have an all-clear in a minute," I say. "Now hang on till I give the signal. Taltus," I call out. "Let me come up to you."

I climb the line past Kalia, pulling Toq up with me, leaving him with his sister as I kick my way through rotten meat-bits, slide my body around a big piece. Looks a bit like a steak.

Bill would laugh. I'm hungry again.

Taltus pulls me close, so our helmets are touching, so my vision is just filled with that bone mask under a visor. I switch off my comm. He does the same.

I speak, letting it vibrate through our helmets.

"Once they get the ship up and out of this mess, them scabs might shoot us. I mean, they're bound to shoot us eventually, but I can't say whether they'll do it now or wait till we've finished the job."

"I will die for you, and the children, if needed."

"That's a fine sentiment, but that en't what we need." Taltus's eyes shine from under that mask. The eyes of a believer. Aiya. It's a good thing he en't in no position to bow.

"Listen," he says. "Listen, Jaqi, there are things you must hear me say, without anyone listening."

This slab going to pledge his fealty to me or some crazing like that? "Taltus—"

"Our swords are different than those given to the Resistance. Beaten steel, by hand, a thousand blows for the thousand blows Saint Thuzera struck against Belial. They are not mass-produced, sss." He takes my hand in his huge clawed one, moves my hand to the sword's hilt. "You see? They are part of us. Each of us."

"Oh . . . kay." Why this, now? In this midst of the butt-guts, hearing each other only by dint of our helmets being up next to the other?

"Each sword, for each adept, is named and remembered on our homeworld. If I fall, Jaqi, you must take my sword to the Llyrixa system. In-system, hold it and speak and the Council will hear you, through our great central blade. You need not fear. They will heed you, once they know you bear the sword of a fallen adept."

"Nothing's gonna happen to you , Taltus."

"They will listen if you come to them, sss." Hisses rattle the glass between our heads. "It has been many years since the Order was at our greatest strength. The Empire and Resistance both cursed us for failing to take a side. More than that, we cursed ourselves, sss. We argued long among ourselves about the meaning of the scriptures, until some of us sought to do what was right nonetheless, and protect the innocent, and, sss, sss . . ." He is breathing heavily. "I sought to fight. I went against the Order by doing so. Now, if I fall, you must convince them to aid the Reckoning."

"So they may or may not agree, and may or may not use their might for our side. Thanks?"

Thing about the religious types—they don't know sarcasm. "You are welcome. Jaqi, remember—what is fated will come to pass, but you must ensure you, and your people, are prepared for it."

I clench my own soulsword. Not sure how well this works through a spacesuit, but it don't matter as I don't get no answer to <u>Araskar, you there?</u>

Nothing. Again.

Up we go.

Taltus pulls us up the line, up, up, us squirming and wiggling through the layers of flesh.

"Ew, ew, ew!" Kalia shouts.

"I figure on steak tonight," I say, and she groans. "Steak and entrails! I like a good bit of entrails."

"Stop it, Jaqi!"

"Don't judge a girl because she likes some entrails."

This is an improvement over the not-talking we been doing, I guess. Back to teasing her.

Taltus's grapnel pulls us through the fleshy bits, up and up—and then, just like that, we pop out the top.

The mining operation is above us. It's all flesh, honeycombed with holes, endless piles of tissue, lit by thousands of ring lights. There's a massive machine in the center, a gravity centralizer that lets folk way up there stand on the "ceiling." Way above us.

We're standing on a pile of butt-guts stuck in the maw of a funnel, a big funnel that sits at the bottom of tunnels and slides and every trash-dumping apparatus I ever done seen.

Other funnels around us are empty, material slipping down into the fire, but our funnel is evil full, stacked up in mountains of this nasty meat.

Taltus hooks me and the kids to the line he's shot. The grappling hook wraps around a metal tube above. Tunnels and stairs all connect to a maintenance door, one of dozens set in the walls of flesh and plasticene.

"Be, sss, careful," Taltus says, getting on the radio. "I see Reveks already coming to check on this incinerator. They must have gotten an update about its failure to operate."

Sure enough, the maintenance door we need to go into opens, and a few little ratlike Reveks scurry out, along metal pilings and fleshy walls both. I take a minute to thank God, or the Starfire, that Shadow Sun Seven didn't trust the Suits with maintenance.

He hands me and the kids the grapnel, lifting us up, toward that metal tube. Once we clamber on top of the tube, out of sight of them Reveks, I take my helmet off. And I'm sorry I did so—it smells evil awful in here, like all the rotting meat in the galaxy mixed with some fresh turds—but I motion for the kids to take off their helmets, so they can hear me, without Matakas listening in.

"Ew, ew, ew, ew," Kalia mutters as we cling to the top of the tube, and Taltus comes up on the grappling hook below, scrambling his big lizard body up to the top of the tube.

"We gotta get in there," I say, pointing to the maintenance door. The Reveks already closed it. "These swords cut through mag-locks, Taltus?"

"Don't worry about it, Jaqi," Kalia says. She raises a funny-looking little bit of tech, a little spidery black thing. "I have the Pet."

"You have the what?" Miss This-Is-Gross-Where's-My-Tea? She's got something to aid the mission?

"I'm not useless," she says, giving me a look that says she knows what I'm thinking. "Let me through."

"All right, then. Never said you was useless, Kalia."

She doesn't look at me. I let her scuttle by on this slick tube. She gets her way up to the tunnel and presses her little pet against it, and the door hums a bit, like the Pet trying to open it.

"Where'd you pick that up?" I ask as we scuttle up to her. Toq climbs in through the tunnel. I can just barely get in there. Taltus—that'll be the trick. He's eyeballing it, looking for all the world like the seven-foot lizard he is.

"The Engineer," Kalia said. "I had a little talk with him when you and Z did takeoff prep, back on the Suits' planet."

Huh. I don't want to tell her that Pet's a Suit of its own notion; probably some organic bits in there to help maximize whatever it does, and if it had a chance, it'd turn her brain into a database. "What'd you give that fella in return?"

"Data. Same thing they always wanted."

"What sort of data?"

She don't answer. The maintenance door slides open and I reckon anyone but the kids'll have a hard time in there. I'm just skinny enough to get in that. Taltus—both Kalia and I turn and look at him.

"I will have to find another way in, sss," he says. "I will not fit."

That's when it all goes to hell.

A roar, a pop, a thunderous explosion—and them pink fleshy bits fly *everywhere,* spattering hot and messy across our suits. More than that, though—metal screams, and sentients scream, and wires and pipes are ripped free. The tube we're standing on rocks, shakes back and forth, and I grab Toq and toss him in that maintenance door, Kalia scrambling in after him, and I fall and slip, and Taltus grabs me to stop me plunging back down into the buttguts.

Our incinerator has just come on—and the Matakas' ship caught in it.

The ship screams and shoots a column of fire high into the mines. Heat washes over me—and then my vision's obscured by the splattering bits.

I yell to Taltus, "Matakas! I thought you told them to

shoot their way out of there!"

"I did, sss. They must not have made it in time." He struggles to get up, to get a foothold on the pipe we're on. It's shaken now, and we're about to slide down. Below us, there's fire still shooting out of the top of the incinerator, the ship's explosion having pretty much ruined everything—the Reveks, those that survived, are doing the little rat-scramble to get back up.

Matakas are dead? Can't say I'm going to miss them, but they was our ride out . . .

And then shards flash down there. All the poor little Reveks who climbed down there to manually activate the incinerator take shards. They scream and join the mess of meat down there. Oh hell.

Matakas, in their own spacesuits, climb up out of the ashes.

They're much reduced, but I recognize Swez's voice screaming at us in the radio. "Female, you betrayed us! We barely escaped our ship in time!"

Of course they did. "It en't my fault, drone—"

I'm hanging half off the pipe, from one of the maintenance handholds, so of course, one of the Matakas fires right at me. The shard hits the pipe, rocks me back and forth. I scramble to the top of this pipe, hug it to try and hide. The handholds are meant for Reveks and I can barely get two fingers hooked in. Taltus's grip is looking even worse, as he tries to dig his claws in through the material of his spacesuit. "I told you, it weren't on purpose, Swez!"

He don't answer.

No more shards come at me, but my perch is getting evil precarious. I stick my head up after a minute. Seems safe. Maybe the Matakas are fighting miners now, or security.

"No!"

Three things go and happen at once.

I slip on the guts that have gone everywhere, and I nearly go tumbling off the pipe. Taltus catches me.

Right below us, a Mataka takes aim, right at my head.

Taltus whips around, and takes a shard full through the back. He falls onto me, twice my weight, pushing me back into the open maintenance tunnel.

Taltus is gagging, and bleeding all over me, the shard still burning in him, having broken up to burn its way through his bone and blood and organs. I look up into his eyes, between the hand-carved holes in the bone of his mask. Blood oozes out from the bottom of his mask, thick black blood dripping down onto my spacesuit.

"Take it," he mutters, and presses the big old handle of his soulsword into my hand. "Tell my people to believe. Jaqi—Saint Jaqi—"

He reaches up, hooks a hand under his mask, and—

Then he's dead.

I nearly scream at the Matakas, but I just stop myself. Somehow, handing off the big old soulsword of Taltus to Kalia, I get into the maintenance tunnel and Kalia closes the door. The mag-locks engage and shards flash outside.

Taltus's body falls into the incinerators.

"They killed him," Kalia says. "They killed Taltus! Those bastards! We should shoot them all!"

I can't find no words.

"How will we get out of here without the Matakas?" Kalia asks.

"Let me do that worrying," I say, gripping tight to Taltus's sword. I don't expect Kalia to take that—figure it's about time she had one of her moments, what where she cries and prays and all that.

Instead, she just nods, and holds her brother, and them tears are silent. "Okay, Jaqi." Kalia touches her head and her chest in that way that church folk do. "I'm sure that Taltus will be . . . he's . . . he's with God. Okay. What should we do now, Jaqi?"

Hell, I just said that on account of I couldn't think of nothing. "We do the mission."

Jaqi

THE KIDS ARE TOO QUIET.

I been around kids a little while now, and I can tell you they don't ever stop making noise, even when they're trying not to. They're always grunting, or whimpering, or crying, or twitching noisy-like. Even when they sleep they flop around and snore and babble.

Not now. These are the quietest kids in all the spaceways. We're sneaking through the cell blocks of Shadow Sun Seven, silent as any trained assassin. I'm holding out the sword Araskar gave me, Taltus's being too heavy. Managed to strap it to my back for now.

<u>Slab, you there? I en't sure where we are—what've you got in your brainpan that could help?</u> He don't answer.

So far, Araskar and Z are useless. Here I am doing the Reckoning's dirty work in the butt-guts. They're up there eating pure thurkuk secretion and Routalais chocolate.

Behind me, a door I hadn't noticed—must be a passageway for guards only—opens right up, and a guard steps out. One of them blobs.

Thought they was supposed to be sick?

The blob's between me and the kids, and they's who he sees, not me.

He's oozing blue mucus, gurgling and making noise like I make when I've drunk way too much, and he raises a dripping tendril, and gurgles something into a translator that says, "Humans? What are you doing out?"

Kalia and Toq don't do a damn thing—they just freeze, stare at the guard.

"Back to the mines." A giant slop of mucus falls off him and splatters on the floor.

I keep waiting for him to see me, but he don't—just focuses on the kids. Them fluid sentients can see out of their whole bodies, but maybe the sickness is making him stupid. Maybe I have a chance, here. Just for a second. He sways slightly, and a couple of drops of mucus ooze from his body to splash on the floor. "How'd you get out without—"

I cross the space between me and the guard and I sink that soulsword of mine deep into the blue oozing flesh. He wails, and his whole body shudders and starts to melt, to try and slide off the sword, but I yank it around, and I must cut something vital, because he shrieks and stops moving and just flattens, oozes—

And then he's a puddle at our feet, goo dripping off the sword. He's dead.

But that en't all of it. No, the soulsword talks to me, all of a sudden.

I felt this before, but it was from a battle-hardened scab of the worst sort; this simple guard's life done rushes into me.

This en't no high-up Imperial lackey, en't no one of no harm. Just a scab needed a job. All his folk did. He got mates and a child; the fluid sentients mate in threes. He is first-mate; his second patrols the market, his third tends the child and fixes broken shard-blasters. Together they manage to survive sleeping in a converted prison cell, and they are saving up to go somewhere better than this hole. It's one of the only places with decent work for fluids, but there's something rotten about it, them prisoners being worked too hard.

Fact is, he knows something funny about the mines. Something going on with the miners—but I forget that, for a minute, when I learn how his child loves it when he brings home olives; they get vat-grown olives in the guards' lounge.

She slurps them right up, when he holds them out on a probiscis.

He won't bring home no olives tonight.

Worst part is, I feel some of his knowledge, about how

to get around down here, will be damned useful. Suddenly I know where we are, I know how to get to the 2000s cell block. Araskar briefed me, but this is much easier.

All that life, and now nothing more than blue goo on the floor and useful intel.

"Jaqi?" Kalia and Toq stare at me, their eyes wide.

Blue goo all over me and all over the floor, that was a sentient until just a moment ago.

"Jaqi, are you okay?" Kalia steps forward. "Jaqi, you're trembling."

"You killed him," Toq says, almost in relief.

"I know what I done, Toq," I snap. "There's still a call out for your heads, you forgot?"

The kids freeze. Aw, hell. "Sorry," I say, and pull them close. "I'm sorry. I ought not to bark."

Toq embraces me. Kalia resists, and after a moment, she starts to babble, "We didn't know, Jaqi! We didn't know what the bluebloods did! We didn't—"

"Shhh," I say. "Don't nobody deserve what was done to you. Come on."

"We didn't know," she babbles.

I may be comforting the kids, but it don't mean a thing to me. It's hard to talk. Somehow I figured, in this prison, they'd all be scabs like the Matakas, what deserve it for one reason or another. This blue fellow's little one won't see him come home. "There's a lift at the end here gonna get us where we want."

The kids run to the lift.

I know I shouldn't look. I shouldn't stare any longer at this puddle of blue goo, what used to be a genuine sentient that just got in my way. But I do stare. I stare a long time, and I think a thousand crazy things in just a few moments, think that I'll go find his child and take care of her.

I wish for a funny thing: I wish I could talk to Araskar, him what might understand what this feels like.

I put my hand on the sword. Slab, you there?

Araskar

This is the morning after we were first together. Difference is, I'm seeing it through Rashiya's eyes.

She's watching me dress. Admiring me as I pull my clothes on. Admiring my vat-grown muscles, every inch of them. No scars, not yet, just the body I've been sweating and shaping in hopes I'll get through the Resistance's first battle. She thinks about running her hands over my chest, clinging to my back, thinks it would be a shame if a body she liked so much won't make it out.

And then she's nervous. Terrified, actually. She didn't have to do this, and here she is, about to go into battle with the same chances I have. Her father told her she had a chance at safety. Her mother begged her not to go.

I wish I could tell my younger self how random the chances are, how all the training won't matter. He'll see everyone die, but he'll duck back into the boarding pod in time, just because he drew the safe spot at the back. An entire platoon. Thirty-nine other people he's laughed and drank and sweated and cursed and prayed with.

But this version of me doesn't know anything. Doesn't know how special he's about to be.

"So, private," Rashiya asks, because she's not willing to say, "Come back to bed for a bit," or any of the tender things she's thinking. "What brought you to the Resistance?"

"Uh, ha." I laugh nervously. When did I ever laugh nervously? Before I'd ever been into battle, it seems. "Everyone in our platoon thought it sounded better than the Dark Zone."

"That's really it?"

"That en't good enough?" When did I ever use spaceways slang? Must have my guard up. Trying to sound like I'm not a cross; we all know perfectly well how to speak because of the data dump in our heads. "What, you were convinced by the Imperial propaganda? *You Aren't Sentient, Because We Need You to Die?*"

"Just wondering," Rashiya says. "Sometimes people have these detailed answers about what they want to do with their lives. I've met quite a few crosses that want to be writers, or artists, or singers. They've got a book planned out, or a ballad of the Resistance. They act like the war's all but won. Like we're not all lined up to die still. I mean, we'll die in the service of something, but it's still death, aiya?" She tries not to sound afraid.

She's so afraid.

She used spaceways slang too. I guess we were both putting up a front. "Have you ever been in a battle?" I ask, from where I stand sliding my shirt over my head.

"Oh, a few."

"How'd a homegrown cross get involved?"

"My folks were . . . agricultural workers." A practiced phrase. "A lot of escapees from the Navy try to blend into the ranks of the farmers. The Empire used to raid the farms and conscript anyone who looked like a military model. It didn't exactly endear me to the Empire."

"They still around?"

"Yes, but they don't know what I'm doing. I'd like to keep it that way."

"Yeah." I stop and look at her. Nervous as hell, I am.

"We'll do this again," she says, "if we're both lucky

enough to come out the other end of this battle." She gets up, and gives me a quick kiss. Not a lot of compassion in it. I try, fumbling to return the kiss, but she steps away. "I'll take that kiss if we survive."

The ghost of Rashiya detaches from the memory-Rashiya, turns and talks to me. "I never said I loved you, did I?"

"You couldn't. I got promoted. The next time you snuck into my bed, you bribed three minor officers to ignore what we were doing."

"Right," she says. "My father hadn't recruited me into black ops yet. And you looked different." Her ghost-hand comes up, to trace the scars on my face.

"I saw battle."

"Seemed stupid to talk about love, after that."

Another one of her memories. Another moment isolated by the war. We're in some sanctum for John Starfire; Rashiya was brought here blind, so that she wouldn't know where her sisters were. She suspects her father had the same done—a soulsword could reveal the location, after all.

It's a nice place. A farm in the hinterlands of Irithessa. Even here in the center of the Empire, they remember a time when a star system had to be self-sufficient. A few hills made purple by the morning mist; wide fields of corn and wheat.

She's standing on the porch talking to her father.

"You've been quiet," he says. "It's about Araskar?"

"Let's not talk about him," she says, and turns her gaze to the wheat fields, a hazy golden stretch in the morning mist.

"We're all lonely in the end, in this business, Rashiya," he says, and touches her arm. "Your sisters don't understand that. Your mother doesn't accept it. But that's what it is. We've been changed by the war, and we can't change back. No matter how you love him, you're both soldiers, and you'll always be broken."

"I know, Dad." She sounds every bit the petulant teenager who doesn't want a pep talk.

"So, you've thought about my offer."

"Black ops."

"You'd outrank Araskar, next time you meet him. Could order him to lick your boots and he'd have to."

She laughs. "I just might, pater." She hesitates. "I'd see more of . . . the ugly side."

"Yes, you would." He stays at the edge of the porch, staring out over the wheat fields. "You know what would happen if we let them go. If we let them poison what we've made."

Them. He won't even say the word *humans.*

"How did he do it?" I ask Rashiya's ghost.

She turns, disengaging from the memory, disengaging

from the world I took from her head. "Do what?"

"How did your father make peace with the Shir? How did he even speak with them?" I try to reach out for her, take the ghost in my arms. "And why did he think it was possible?"

She doesn't answer. Ghosts don't answer.

Slab, you there? The words careen around the inside of my head.

An orchestra rises up, playing a lumbering, twisting song. I didn't even realize I had my hand on my soulsword's hilt. I try to stumble to my feet and my body twists painfully against the locker they've shoved me into.

I'm here, Jaqi. What's going on?

In the cell block, aiya. Near to the 2000s on the lift. Should have this fellow ready any second now. Getting out'll be a trick, though . . .

Z and X have really packed me in here. I've got to draw my short sword, and I'm having no luck.

Slab, something wrong?

No. Maybe. Why is getting out a trick? The Matakas aren't waiting for the barge?

No, they en't waiting. Their ship's had a situation.

What happened?

Incinerator juiced up too soon. Most of Swez's scabs got out, but they lost some, and now Swez blames me.

<u>Lost Taltus, ai. One of them Kurguls done took him out.</u>
  <u>Shit.</u>
  <u>That right there is a fine word for it.</u>
  <u>We'll have to steal one of the barge loaders, the big ones. We used them to smuggle troops in the Resistance. They can pass in and out of a node. Would have been easier just to rope and steal the barges, but it is what it is.</u> Sounds like Jaqi's half of the plan is going out the airlock as much as my half. <u>I have a problem here too.</u>
  <u>What's going on?</u>
  <u>Z and X want to kill the prison warden.</u>
  That dumbfounds Jaqi for a moment—which, given how talky she normally is, is quite a feat. <u>What'd he ever do to them?</u>
  <u>Killed a raft of Zarra, it seems.</u> I manage to get my small soulsword mostly drawn. I push the sheath against the wall and pull, until I feel the blade come free at last. <u>They won't leave until they kill him. It's suicide to try.</u>
  <u>I told that dumb slab to keep himself alive! He promised!</u>
  <u>He's not keeping that promise.</u>
  <u>He en't getting a kind word from me ever again! I done brought him back to life!</u>
  And then the crazy thing—I can hear her *crying.* Jaqi. Crying. <u>Are you—</u> The music shifts, in a bittersweet, breaking melody that climbs over jagged chords. And it

starts to detune, notes blending as if they're off from each other. Same way as when she ran away before.

Araskar, I can't—this mission, it's all gone to hell. I killed a fella. A poor security fella never done nothing. I wouldn't have known about him, but I done killed him with the soulsword and . . . didn't deserve to get stabbed in the back! Look at me! How've I got any better claim than John Starfire?

I know this feeling. Damn, do I ever. Jaqi, I know. I know that too well.

How we supposed to do the right thing when I done killed an innocent? I was trying to save the innocent.

It'll never leave you. That's not what I meant to say. I meant to tell her she was protecting the kids, no doubt, it's all right, and she should focus on the mission, on keeping them alive. Instead, I find myself thinking of everyone I ever killed. It'll tear you apart. It'll make you want to kill your own insides with drink, with drugs, make you afraid to have any friends ever again. I twist my arm around backward, manage to scrape the point of the sword against the locker door.

That . . . en't a comfort. The music rattles and lumbers, different instruments out of time with each other.

Wasn't supposed to be. My mouth is still dry. My head pounds, demanding more pinks. You find some way to live with it. I'm not sure what that is yet.

<u>Don't want to live with it, slab! Don't want to become one of those who live with it.</u>

<u>Then you'd better change everything, like they say you're going to. I don't know any other way to live.</u>

Jaqi doesn't answer that. But the music starts to come back together, instruments harmonizing, finding the beat.

I shove my arm up. Cramps run from my fingers to my shoulder, but I manage to get a little leverage behind the short soulsword, shove it through the metal, and cut down, until I can kick out a square of metal, until I can shove myself through the bottom of the door.

<u>You okay? What you doing now, Araskar?</u>

I don't get to answer, because the NecroSentry is waiting for me.

-14-

Jaqi

"JAQI, IS THIS THE ONE?"

"Huh?" I release my grip on the soulsword, and my head immediately relaxes without Araskar's words working a jackhammer on the inside of my skull.

"This one." Kalia taps the latest maintenance hatch they've opened. There's a tiny tunnel inside, won't fit no one but the smallest sentient.

"That's the one. Controls the mag-locks." Guard's memory confirms it.

These is high-security cells, the tightest I ever seen. Each one takes up a whole block, has a series of interlocking doors that show us nothing but metal. Whoever this fella is, the Empire wanted to shut them up for a long old time.

"So, wow," Kalia says, looking down the hall. "This person survived a year in the Dark Zone and then scared the Empire so much they got locked away here? What kind of person can do both of those things?"

"Two damn good questions," I say.

"What does he say about it?" She nods toward the soulsword.

For half a second I almost say, *that slab's in more trouble than us,* then I figure these kids got enough on their minds. "He en't, uh, well educated in such things."

Kalia and Toq peer up a maintenance shaft, one too small for anything but kids or Reveks. There's a central bit of tech up there. Kalia squirms up again, climbs back down. "Twenty-four sixteen. Toq, I need you to get up there and put this on it. I can't fit."

Toq takes the thing they called the Pet, frowns at it. "The Suits are creepy," he says, in that weird sort of kid-neutral tone. "I don't like this."

"Toq, this is the most important part of the mission." She's a bit burned off at her brother. "Get up there and do it, aiya!"

We both stare at her. Kalia's talking spaceways?

She flushes. "I said get up there, Toq! It's now or never."

"Why are you talking like Jaqi? You said that Jaqi doesn't talk properly."

Kalia flushes red. "None of this is proper! Why are we arguing about this now? Get your little butt up there!"

He crawls in and Kalia flushes red and won't look at me.

"You picking up bad habits, ai?"

"I didn't mean to treat you the way I did, on the moon of Trace, Jaqi," she says, real slow-like. "I . . . I think maybe the bluebloods are getting what we deserve."

"What? No." Despite the blue goo all over me, despite the moment, I put an arm around the poor kid. "Kalia. Don't believe that. Don't ever believe that."

"I can't help it," she whispers, tucking her head into the crook of my neck. "So many bad things happen. They have to happen for a reason. God must be punishing us, or the Starfire, or something . . ."

"Naw," I say, and clutch her close. "Girl, please don't think that. We all inherit some share of shit."

"But you ran away!"

That hurts a bit. "I shouldn't have. It was a damn fool action. I didn't know what to do, what with everyone expecting a miracle, and miracles not being easy to do."

She cries again, into my shirt, not noticing all the fleshy bits and blue goo she gets on her face. "If bluebloods don't deserve this, why is it happening?"

That I don't have an answer for. "Hell, honey, the galaxy spins the wheel of crap for everyone. Been a long time since your people were in the shit, but it just happens to be your turn."

"I can't believe that. Everything happens for a reason."

"Can you believe the reason en't your fault?" Her

tearstained, blood-and-goo-stained face looks up at me. "Can you believe that maybe the reason en't got a thing to do with you, and you was caught in its wake?"

She makes a funny face, and goo drips off her slanted eyebrow. "Are you telling me not to be so self-centered?"

Toq hollers, "Okay, it's open!"

Kalia wipes away tears, and leaves grime spread across her cheeks and forehead.

We head down the hall to 2416. This is it.

The mag-locks are still slowly disabling, and then we trip the manual levers that open the door. Central lock spins, and the doors part.

And there inside, is the scab we done gone to all this trouble for, sitting cross-legged, quiet and still.

And this scab . . . huh.

Skinny. Could be human. Could be a cross, if a design I en't seen before. Like Araskar, it's clear that this one could handle a fight. Shaved head, slitted eyes, thick ropes of muscle under the tanktop.

Got a couple of tubes running out of a couple of flesh pockets just above the waist, under a standard prison-issue shirt. The flesh tubes run into the walls.

I can't put no female nor male to this one. That's a bit unusual for a cross. Can't tell the original model, neither. I reckon the word is *viiself,* which is what humanoids who en't male nor female go by. Them folk say vi, vir, vimself in place of the hes and shes.

Vi is awake. I see green eyes between them slits. I wonder about them tubes coming out of vir chest, running into the walls. We got a sentient needs feeding tubes here? Kalia sticks the Pet on the walls' control panels, looking to open whatever the tubes go to.

"Salutes, scab. They feeding you out of a tube?" I ask vim. Those eyes, them bright slits, almost make vim look like something other than a cross. Something more like a cat.

Kalia says, "Do you think it's okay to approach vim?"

Vi speaks, voice croaking a bit. "Two soulswords? So many enemies, aiya?"

Hey, how bout that—this scab speaks spaceways, like me.

Vi blinks, and speaks again in that croaky voice. "We need water, aiya."

En't no one else in here, but hell, I reckon long enough in the dark and I'd have plenty of friends in my own head, so that explains this *we*.

I detach the water store from my suit and hold it up to vir lips. Vi sucks it greedily.

Vir long-fingered hands are shackled. Not just shackled with an energy shackle, but crossed with wire and bound tightly. I take out a shard-cutter, a simple tool in my suit, but the kind of thing spells freedom for this type.

Vir eyes go a bit wide, I reckon, thinking about getting vir hands free. I don't cut yet. "You the one lived a year inside the Dark Zone, aiya?"

Them eyes get wider, no longer so slitted and suspicious. I done surprised vim. "Who sent you? The Resistance? John Starfire finally figured he'd pay mind to us?"

"Not the Resistance. The Reckoning."

Vi says, "What in space is the Reckoning?"

Aw, I felt so grand saying it, too. Well, give it time for the word to get around. "En't got time to explain," I say. "You lived a year in the Dark Zone; we're after information about the devils. You got it, I get you out." I thumb the controls for the shard-cutter, let it flash a little red.

"Oh, we have it," vi says.

"What is it?"

"We knows plenty, scab," vi says, "that we will say as soon as we have our selves all back in our hands."

"Your selves?"

Just then, Kalia finishes her trick with the Suits' Pet and the sides of the cell slide open—to reveal that the tubes vi is talking about go to a couple of—

"Guns?" Kalia stares back at vim. "You have an organic connection to guns?"

Yep, two silver, fine-looking pistols, all levers and locks, the kinds of things I coulda fenced just a few months back and got my own asteroid for the catch. The organic tubes feed right into the bottom of the gun's handles. Never seen a thing like that before.

"Them's our other selves, girl." Vi smiles, showing small, white teeth. "Skithrr symbionts, last two in existence, run my pistols. We been cast out of lots of places for it, but we en't never failed each other."

"You're—" Kalia's eyes flash between vim and me, as if I'm supposed to get something. "You're—you're—Jaqi, this is—"

I wait, but she done run out of words. "Yeah, girl?"

Splutter. Stare. Splutter.

"Kalia, you're going to have to spit some words before your head explodes."

And then, at long last, some words. "This is Scurv Silvershot!"

"What? No." I star at vir hands, them I was about to cut free. "That fella en't real." Scurv Silvershot, in them holos Bill used to watch every damn night? I got them holos things memorized, but that Scurv didn't look nothing like this one. Lot handsomer, for one thing. All scruffy and rugged. This one has the look of a cat; all ready to spring and kill, and sure, vi's pretty, but in a way kind of scares me.

"You en't no legend," I say.

"Real," vi says in that creaky voice, and now we all listen. "We're the greatest shot in the galaxy. Nailed the

Tyrant of Eridess right between the eyes from orbit. Flew between the twin suns of Sikaaria and only got singed. Saw the collection of Muracoon the Mad, and were nearly added to it. Fought Ariel Singh across the wild worlds. Recently returned from the Dark Zone." Vi swallows dryly and adds, "Shitty place."

"Like the comic books!" Toq says.

Vi scowls. "Don't talk about them comic books. Them owes us money."

"Hang it, now, how you supposed to prove you're the greatest shot in the galaxy?" I ask.

"Guess you oughta put them guns in our hands, girl."

Kalia is giving me this look. And it's a funny look, let me tell you, like she thinks I know what to do with Scurv Silvershot vimself, like I'm going to say something makes sense of this whole situation and what to do with a real-life comic book fella in the guts of a Ruuzan Threg prison.

"What'd they get you for, scab?"

"Copyright infringement," Scurv says, and vir lip curls up in anger.

"Say what? Copyright?"

"They think they can tell us how to live with them damn comic books."

"That en't the whole story. Can't be."

"What do you know about the Dark Zone?" Kalia

asks. "We were told you survived a year in there. We were only there a few minutes when the . . . when *they* tried to devour us."

Vi sighs, and stretches, twists vir neck. Again, like a cat. "Oh, we've seen the devils. Flew right past their hungry mouths. And we know there's a planet and star, sitting right in the center of the Dark Zone, that them devils don't touch."

There's a planet right in the center of the Dark Zone? Say what? "Them devils eat planets and suns."

"The Shir leave this solar system alone."

I'm so rattled by this I forget to tell vim not to name the devil. "Folk live there? On this planet?"

"They do," Scurv says, and gives a little smile and shake of the shoulders, but vir eyes don't change. "Planet called TS-101. It had another name, once. No one but us knows that, and that, we tells you once we're out of here."

"TS-101 en't no designation I ever heard."

"Aiya, girl. It's an old First Imperial designation. Changed a thousand years ago. The universe lives and dies by file clerks, ai?"

"You could find it again?"

Vi shrugs. "We must say, in truth, that finding it were pure luck. But you could find it, could you track down an old enough map. Pre-Imperial Dark Zone star-designates. Tough to find, but maybe in one of them memory-crypts on Irithessa."

Kalia and I exchange a look, one of them looks where both of us figure there might just be something to this destiny business. "We have one of them maps."

Vi holds vir hands out. "We can take you there, you show us this map. Just let us out. Let us hold each other again." Vir eyes flash on them guns. "Please."

Kalia decides it's time to speak up again. "We're fighting against John Starfire. He's lost his mind."

"That's this Reckoning? You're trying to stop John Starfire's crazing. You and these kids?"

"That's what this is," I say. "The Chosen One decided he'd kill every human in all the spaceways."

Vi looks over me, Kalia and Toq, and I know what vi's thinking. "I reckon you're just getting this Reckoning started."

"Aiya, well, we got some more folk with us." I leave out the bit where other folk are having more trouble. "Could use a professional gun-toter, truth. How you feel about old John Starfire?"

"Well, now, a scab in our position'd say anything to get out, aiya?" Vi gives a laugh, a laugh sounds genuine. I reckon strange things happen to a sense of humor in the lonelies here. "But we did meet John Starfire. Wasn't what he called himself then."

"And?"

"We reckon by then he'd killed plenty, and was going to kill plenty more, and he told himself what he had to so's he could live with all them bodies he put down."

Okay, that right there I know to be true words.

I start cutting vir bonds. Scurv Silvershot, welcome to the Reckoning.

15

Araskar

THE NECROSENTRY SHOVES ME against the glass. On the holo, Z and X roar their triumph to the crowd. They were supposed to fight each other, in an elaborate re-creation of a jungle world. Instead, they've stopped, and are holding their weapons up, waving them at Boss Cross.

Boss Cross wipes his brow. "You're lucky we have some medication that helped me recover from your, heh, dosage." He just touches the shock stick to me, and my whole body convulses in pain. "I'm tempted to force-feed you the pinks, but I need you talking."

I look over at the holo. Z and X bellow something unintelligible. I can guess what it is. *Fight us, Faceless Butcher!*

"But you knew that, didn't you? Araskar."

Shit. Even more than the pain, there's the realization that he knew my name. And that maybe he left the soulswords out as bait. "What—" I groan through the words. "What do you know?"

"Not as much as you do, it seems. I got an answer from John Starfire himself."

Like I feared.

"Why does John Starfire want a nobody like you so badly? Whatever caused you to cut and run on Swiney, and bring the head of the Resistance after you?" The soulsword's shard edge pressed against my back, a line of pain down the spine. "I'd like to know that story. Although I feel all you'll get from me is a *cutting* remark."

"Memory's blade cuts deepest of all, yes?" Rashiya's ghost says.

I actually laugh, even twisted half to death as I am.

"You laughed at my joke," the Boss says.

The NecroSentry turns me around and the Boss squints at me through those nondescript eyelids.

"You laughed. No one ever laughs at my jokes."

"It was a great joke," I say, and am glad my face is so bruised, because even I can't keep a straight face with a lie like that.

The NecroSentry whacks me again, quadrupling my headache, and grunts, "Death."

He nods to the NecroSentry. "Have the Zarra zoom on up. We'll explain to them that they work for me now. They can say good-bye to their old manager, whatever he wants, because he's going back to the Resistance."

"They will try to kill you," the NecroSentry growls.

He shrugs. "Think of all the blood and honor when you break their legs and implant obedience chips in them."

And then he shoves that micro-shard stinger into my back. Just for a moment—but it's enough to blast my entire nervous system, release whatever's in my bladder and leave me nose-down in drool.

When I come to, I see my clients.

Z and X bring a mighty stink into the Boss's office. They're covered in blood and mud, bits of other sentients.

They can't help but notice that I'm lying in the middle of the floor, my muscles still twitching, unable to move. My hands won't do what they tell me to. Z, X, and the NecroSentry swim in my vision. The only steady figure in my field of vision is Rashiya's ghost.

"Welcome. Have a drink of water," the Boss says.

They both stare at him.

"Or don't." The Boss gets up, walks around me. "It seems the Resistance wants your manager very badly. I've had to detain him. So here is the deal. You both work for me. Fights are once a week. All expenses paid and provided for, but you don't leave Shadow Sun Seven. You make it a year, you are free to retire, or sign again for a significant offer."

"We came to fight you honorably," Z says.

"Not this again," the Boss says.

"We are not afraid to die, Faceless Butcher!" Z roars, and steps closer—until the NecroSentry seizes his shoulder. I'm impressed with the monster's grip, on both myself and Z.

"Come and fight us," X says. "Your monster may hurt us, but we will die in honor."

"Eh," the Boss says with all the emotion of someone who's just been told something inconsequential. "I suppose we have to talk about that. Very well. Protest and I activate my contacts on your homeworld."

"Your contacts?" X says.

"We have come to make you pay for your crimes, to bring you death in the deepest dishonor, to—" Z is halfway through his prepared speech when the Boss's words sink in. "What are you speaking of?"

"I still have agents placed on the Zarra's homeworld, and this includes a few xenobiologists who have access to very privileged information. Notably, they have access to a rarified form of the digger virus. You remember the digger virus, I think."

"I was just a child when it struck," X says.

"But you remember. Your people always do. That is all they can do—remember. Heh." That dry, humorless laugh. "How would you like to see another bout of it? See your proud people, your elders, your children, turned mad and digging in the ground until their fingers turn to stubs. Until they forget to eat, forget to drink water." He says it all in that flat, bored tone. "I killed a lot of Zarra, but I can always kill more."

"Curse you, and all your ancestors, and curse—" Z defaults to his practiced speech, until the NecroSentry lets go of my arm and uses that hand to cover his mouth.

I immediately try to stand—and crumple, my nerves still not obeying due to the shock stick.

"So you will belong to me, yes? Or do you need a little more time to grandstand?"

X gives me a hand, and I manage to get to my feet, though I suspect my legs won't hold me up.

"It is not an honorable proposal," X says.

"Zarra are so peculiar," the Boss says, "and yet so predictable. It's clearly documented that the first of your people are crosses, genetically modified humanoids, who changed yourself to tolerate the toxins in the air and water of your planet. It's a terrible place. Absolutely *toxic* personalities, heh. Yet you haven't been there a few hundred years before you decide that you evolved on that terrible world, and you had been there forever, and all other sorts of nonsense."

"You will die screaming—" Z bellows.

"You will work for me," he says. "Let the Sentry take

you back to your quarters and let you relax while I take care of this manager. Or attack, and damn your people."

X holds me up, her iron-hard arms around my midsection and keeping me from slumping, as my vision is still spotty from the beating. She has hardly moved.

And then, in one movement, she drops me and tosses a knife.

The NecroSentry is fast, but not fast enough. The knife glances off the Boss's head, leaving a uniquely bloody eye and bloody slash down the rest of his boring face. He stumbles back. "Wha—"

"Better that every Zarra die than you violate any of our people's honor." X steps over me. The NecroSentry swings a massive fist at her midsection, sends her flying against the wall. To do it, though, the Sentry relaxes his grip on Z, who tears off one of the massive fingers and wriggles out.

Boss comes up bleeding, and even through my blurry vision, there is a half second where Z almost gets him. Z is damn fast, and springs up, over the chair, his hand out, his claws extended—

The Boss jabs a shock stick into Z's chest. Wave after wave of the shocks pulse through Z and he screams. He shakes and screams. He reaches for the Boss, his arm shaking, drool spinning out of his mouth, the floor and the nice couch wet with his urine. He still reaches. With one hand he reaches, and one other shaking hand grabs the shock stick, tries to crush it.

Any other sentient would give up and die.

Instead, Z breaks the shock stick. It snaps with a screaming whine and a loud roar of pain from Z.

The NecroSentry picks up Z and slams him to the ground next to me.

Through a new haze of pain, I hear the Boss say, "Put them back into the ring. With the meanest thing we have."

16

Jaqi

SCURV STANDS UP. Vi walks to the right, picks up one gun, and lets out a shudder, a shake through vir entire body. Goes to the other gun, does the same thing. "We are together, again. My lovelies." Scurv tucks them guns into a couple of skin pockets that expand, like holsters. Them tubes shrink away, but I reckon they'll pop out again when vi needs them. "We are feeling good about this prison break. Who have we the pleasure of working with, in this Reckoning?"

"Jaqi," I say.

"Kalia and Toq, of Formoz, or the Keil Hallits."

"Formoz's brood?" Scurv half smiles. "We remember your pater when he was but a cub."

"Oh, that's nice that you knew Dad," Kalia says.

"Stole a shipload of nukes right from under his nose, we did."

Kalia don't seem nearly as delighted about that. "Come on. Jaqi, where are we going now?"

"Araskar didn't disable none of the main mag-locks between cell blocks and the upstairs. Our best chance of getting out is through the mines." Here it comes. I don't see no way around it. "We got to try talking sense into Swez and them Matakas."

"Not them!" Kalia says. "They killed Taltus!"

"I don't like it," I say, "but they're our best chance of getting this fella off this rock. Well, them, and the comic book star here." I elbow Scurv.

Vi frowns, a frown worthy of a Zarra. "Them comic books lie."

There's a secret entrance to the mines on this level—2666 en't no cell, but don't no one but the guards know it, and me now. I stand there and enter the code, and it opens up, showing a ladder mounted on one of the fleshy ribs, them struts that support the exoskeleton of this big bug.

Up above us, the mines, a labyrinth of cut tissue and the hyperdense oxygen cells. Endless tunnels and chambers of tissue and gleaming cells. Somewhere in there, a loading bay where we can steal barges to get back to Trace.

"You want us to take the lead?" Scurv asks.

"I reckon I got enough swords to deal with trouble," I say, motioning to both my blades. "Watch our backs, though."

"The gravity's weird," Toq says, as we go up.

He's right. The ladder twists and turns, but no matter which way we go, gravity is pushing us against the ladder, so after a minute we all stand up, and walk on the ladder.

"I feel weird, Jaqi," Toq says.

"Too close to the grav generator," Scurv says. "Gets into the bones."

The ladder straightens out into a sort of path, laid with mag-track for some cart that'll come through and pick up the hyperdense cells. Lots of them been mined and set here for pickup. Little, round, shining things, ranging in size from the width of my fist to the size of Toq. Marbles, set into the miles of lung tissue up here. "Keep them hands off your blasters there, Scurv Silvershot," I say. "Stray shot'll blow this place right up."

"We don't miss," Scurv says.

"That's what them comics say too. Thought them comic books lied."

"Not about that."

Mining equipment is everywhere here, from simple cutters—just sharp edges, no shards involved—to whole presses. The equipment lies abandoned. Reckon the prisoners have revolted with the guards sick. And up here, the slime from the poor sick blobs is everywhere. There's a guard platform overlooking this track, dripping with the blue slime. A blob has left bits of itself on the railing for the cart.

We pass one of the blobs, and I motion the kids to hide while Scurv and I scope it out—but the poor thing has just nestled into a cove, a small hollow that a hyperdense cell was cut out of. Thank all gods and goshes this one en't a threat. It's basically poured itself into the cove to try and maintain its shape, and is blubbering softly, sounding a bit like a human snoring with a bad set of sinuses. Its blue, faintly glowing form stands out against the pink pocket of lung tissue.

Reminds me too much of that fellow I killed.

"Will they die?" Scurv asks.

"They en't supposed to," I say. "Matakas promised it would just make them sick for a while."

"If they do, though, we still have what we want." Scurv shrugs.

I don't like that at all. I already killed one poor guard weren't causing anyone trouble—what if I done caused the deaths of all of them? How's that make me different than John Starfire?

"The pathogen will pass, we think. If it is what we think it is, then if it were strong enough to fully discorporate fluid sentients, we would all be having vicious hallucinations. In that, your Matakas stuck to their word."

"Matakas. I reckon I ought to talk to them."

"We have dealt with all the nests," Scurv says. "We

would not have chosen Mataka to work with."

I switch on the comm. "Swez."

"Female? Female cross?" He sounds genuinely surprised on the comm. "You talk with me, now?"

"Don't you do that. You shot Taltus. Shot one of our own party."

"I had nothing to do with that. The drone who shot the Thuzerian has been dispensed with."

Should I believe it? En't like they care much for each other. And it en't like Kurguls need less encouragement to get trigger-happy in a fight. Entirely possible he's telling the truth.

I en't got much of a choice, do I? If I take his word for it, then we have a ride outta here. Otherwise we go out the airlock. I keep talking as we follow the mag-track, hear another sick guard gurgling down the hall. "I didn't have nothing to do with the ship, Swez. That was just bad timing. Look, we'll steal us a few barges, steal one of them big loaders . . ."

"Already done. Barge-man bribed. He'll take us home, for his cut."

I breathe a sigh of relief. Okay, well, maybe this en't going quite as far out the airlock as I thought. "Excellent, scab. We'll meet you there.

"About that," Swez says. I hear quite a few vestigial wings rattling in carapaces in the background.

"What now, scab?"

"Not that we haven't enjoyed our time with you, female, but we are about ten seconds away from the node."

"What?"

"We have a barge-loader full of hyperdense oxygen cells. We have achieved our objective."

I can't even figure on the words to say.

"Some drones thought we should keep you, to sell back to the Resistance. One said it was bad business, but we all agreed that you will be in the Resistance's pocket eventually, and so we weren't offending a potential repeat client. I thought you had potential. Argued to give you a chance. The nest queen agrees. She told us to leave a couple of barges on the platform for you, and that other cross. You should thank me."

"You damned, dirty Kurgul bastards!"

"Come on now, female, surely you can come up with something more original than that." There is a noise in the background, and Swez says, "Salutes, female cross. We are at the node now."

I yell every filthy word I learned in any humanoid or cricket language, but there is a roar and then static as the shortwave comm is cut off. The only way to get ahold of Swez now would be the pure-space relay.

And I don't know his number.

The kids have heard me. "Jaqi?"

I lift the helmet off, exposing my nose to the stink of the mines. "We need to find a new ride."

Araskar

The NecroSentry stands at the edge of the pit. Wearing my soulswords, the bastard. He flashes us a big, stump-toothed smile, and mouths the word *death*. We're stuck in a few painted plasticene "rocks," on sand made from silica bits, the fighting pit all set up to resemble a nice ghastly desert. Very little cover.

"Araskar," X says. "The NecroSentry holds your blades. Can he hear Jaqi?"

"No," I say. "The soulsword's attuned to my psyche. For him it's just a sword. Doing him about as much good now as it does me."

"Did Jaqi tell you anything of use?"

"That she was in trouble too."

"I see."

X has recovered enough to help me stand, and seems little the worse for wear for the NecroSentry's blow. Z, though, is still lying puddled in a heap on the ground, twitching from the effect of the shock stick. He could be like that for the rest of his life. He could recover enough to walk, but continue pissing himself. It's no life for a warrior like him.

"Zarag-a-Trrrro-Rr-Zxz, do you hear me?" She bends over him and whispers a few words into his ear.

"If we get him to a good neuro-reconstructionist in the next day we can save him from a lifetime like this."

"Do not underestimate Zarag-a-Trrrro-Rr-Zxz, Araskar Cross. He will recover."

I don't say anything. It's a nice thought, but no humanoid will recover from a shock stick used like that.

The NecroSentry signals something. The loudspeakers are roaring, but here in the pit, it doesn't come through clearly. "Zarra have . . . Manager, a hero of the war . . . to fare against the Maata!"

I know I've said this a lot lately, but: oh, shit.

The gate opens, and the Maata emerges.

"That is our threat?" X asks. "This is not even on par with the Slinkers."

It's a horned cat, nearly as tall in the shoulders as the NecroSentry. Liquid red eyes glisten in sleek features, and it lets out a low thrumming that fills the arena.

X actually laughs. "This is no task designed to finish off two honorable Zarra."

"No," I start to say, "you don't understand—" But she's off. She clambers to the top of a nearby rock.

The Maata ignores her, slowly winding between the fake rocks, eyes focused on Z and I.

"Z," I say, and take his twitching arm. "Come on buddy, let's get you—" Where? There will be maintenance tunnels under this pit. And they'll lead down to the oxygen works, where we can actually sabotage this place.

"You're just delaying yourself now," Rashiya's ghost says. "Come over to me. You know you want to be with me."

I ignore her. Z grumbles something through his tongue.

X leaps from rock to rock, quietly, after the Maata.

It sure would be nice to tell her why that's not going to work. Not that the Zarra listen.

I manage to drag Z, which is like dragging a spaceship, and also leaving a clear trail for the Maata.

Come on, come on, maintenance tunnel. My guess would be that it's under a rock, that one of these rocks has some kind of lock system that, once undone, allows it to swing out of the way.

No, wait—

I can feel it. It must be all these years of using a soulsword. There's a psychic resonator—under a rock nearby. The rock's big, but I can shift it. I shove the rock as hard as I can, and I see a control panel almost hidden by the fake silica dirt.

A psychic resonator, but keyed to only a few people. Specifically keyed to the blobs, letting them into the maintenance tunnel below the pit via their psychic signature. Still, psychic resonators are strongest when keyed to only one person. The multiple guards and maintenance workers will have thrown this one off. If I had my soulsword, I might even be able to hack it.

I definitely don't have my soulsword.

A growl interrupts my thoughts.

The Maata is close enough to smell now, a musky, thick scent that's a bit like old, stinking mud. Its horns are gleaming, possibly rubbed with a slow-acting poison.

Its eyes focus on us and it lets out a soft purr.

X bellows, "For honor!" and cracks the sense-whip she used as a rope back on the moon of Trace.

She leaps onto its back, and it rears up, and she lashes the whip around its neck and pulls, to garrot the thing.

The Maata doesn't choke. Doesn't make a noise. It rolls sideways, and X has to leap backward to keep from being smeared on a rock—and her makeshift noose goes right through the creature's skin, out its neck, leaving X holding a looped rope.

The cat, apparently unhurt, growls at her.

"It does not bleed?" X says.

"That's not actually a cat!" I yell. "Maatas are blobs.

Fluids, same as the guards!" Story goes that ages ago, a terraforming crew was horrified to find out they'd wiped out the native fluid organism. Then a rather fierce and versatile predator showed up, and they discovered the fluids had survived the terraforming—and evolved to fit into the new ecosystem.

"It is a fluid?"

"A fluid that really likes to look like a big scary cat!"

It chooses that moment to rear up. Its forepaws lose their shape, extend like the blobs' tendrils, and become arms, long, clawed arms. It runs forward on its back legs, hissing still like a cat.

"This is an honorable challenge after all!" she yells as she runs.

"Oh, that's good news!"

"Get up, Zarag—aghh!"

The Maata has connected. X rolls away. She disappears behind rocks, but the Maata has now re-formed to run faster, and I hear her bellows as it gives her more blood to go with her honor.

I bring my fist down onto the control panel and am rewarded with a feeling like a spike into the base of my brain. Everything goes black and when I blink I'm face-down in the silica.

The psychic resonator has a serious backlash.

"Araskar." Z manages to hold his head up. He lifts a

shaking arm, one painstaking inch at a time. "Take this. There is—ahhhh—still a charge."

He's got the broken-off end of the shock stick in his hand.

I don't ask questions; I just grab it. These things work by heating up a miniature shard that creates an electrical current through the nervous system of the the poor recipient; if the shard is still heated it might overload this thing.

If I can stand the pain from the psychic resonator.

I jam the end of the shock stick down into the control panel. Feels like hot mercury poured through my spinal cord.

I twist the stick, my teeth gritted against the pain, my whole body seizing up.

Rashiya dances before my eyes, her green eyes and red hair bright against the haze of darkness from the pain. "Are you ready to die yet?" I can feel her hand in mine. Dry, callused from swordfighting. "You have to be ready by now! Come on! There's no more music left! There's nothing left! You must be ready to die!"

"Araskar!"

Z pulls me away and I look down to see the control panel sparking. With a shaky hand, Z manages to wedge his claws under the panel and tear it out.

The sound I wanted comes up through the new

opening—the roar of the oxygen works underneath the fighting pits.

"X!" I try to stand, and stumble.

X is dodging the Maata, currently a half biped again, running on short, bowed legs, with long arms reaching for her. It lowers its head to charge at her, and she actually dashes forward, and just rolls under its charge, between its legs, springs to her feet and runs away, toward us.

I try to help Z into the tunnel, and he shoves me away. "You go first," he says, spit hanging on the edge of his lip. "It is the coward's way, and you have no honor."

"Nice to see you're feeling better."

17

Jaqi

"WE NEED ANOTHER RIDE?" Kalia says. "Another ride?"

"The Matakas took off."

Toq wrinkles up his little head, too confused to be shocked. "They already went home?"

I would evil like to fall over and curl up into a ball. And maybe weep for a week.

Problem is, all three of my crew, even the legendary sheriff of the wild worlds, are looking at me for an answer.

"He said they left a couple of barges for us."

"Not much thrust on those barges. It will take a few days to cover the distance the barge-loader covers in minutes. Unless we can commandeer another loader ship," Scurv says.

"Well, we en't hurting for oxygen, if we can get a good sense-field going in the barge. We'll just pop one of them cells . . ." I leave out the part where the cells have to be carefully tapped to avoid an explosion, and I en't got the equipment. One insane disaster of a mission at a time, aiya?

"So we can get out of here?" Kalia says.

"Don't you worry," I say. I don't want to ever hear her cry that she deserves this. "I'll get us out."

"Let us follow this track, then," Scurv says, and although I en't know vim long, I would say, even without the holos, that's vir "forcing cheerful" voice.

We keep walking, following the mag-track. It gradually opens up, into a main shipping chamber where several mag-tracks meet. A huge heap of them hyperdense cells reaches up one vast, ragged pink wall to our left. Another giant heap to our right. Overhead, curtains of them cells hang.

I en't never seen such wealth. Three of them cells would have set me up for a year, in the time before the kids.

There en't no carts buzzing back and forth, though. This catch is just sitting right here, waiting for the right hands. Blue slime is everywhere too, but what blobs we see are sick, nestling into hollows to try and retain their shape.

"Jaqi."

Toq is tugging my arm. "Jaqi! I know him!"

"Know who? Someone here?"

"Him!"

I didn't see them until now. The miners. Toq is pointing at one of the miners.

They were hiding in the curtains of tissue. Ragged

types, most of them looking underfed, clad in hazard suits that have seen better days. They're all clustered around the equipment, staring at us like we're going to kill them. Now they've noticed us, they're looking ready to scatter—a good thought, given that Scurv, despite all my words, is still touching them guns.

Wait a touch.

They're all human.

All of them.

I thought this was a prison for all the scabs and the troubled crosses of the galaxy. Why am I seeing a bunch of humans, could all be bluebloods by the look?

And one of them staring at Toq and Kalia, and his face has the look of a fella seen the face of the devil and God both. "Kalia? Toq? My . . ."

"Uncle Staran?" Kalia runs forward. "I thought you were dead!"

"I *knew* you were dead! I saw the reports! What are you—why are you *here*?"

They rush into his arms, this skinny, bald fella!

"Uncle?" I say. I look at Scurv, as if vi will understand this any more than me. "Uncle? Here?"

He looks up, from between the children, at me. "What are you doing here? What is this—" He seems to recognize me, and gets the look of Scurv as well, and his voice goes much darker. "Why are you with *crosses*?"

For a skinny fella on the verge of death, he can definitely stare the Dark. "We en't with the Resistance," I say. "We're set against them."

"Who are you? You are crosses—but you're not with the Resistance?"

"We're the Reckoning," Scurv says.

Oh, see, that sounds evil exciting.

"Who are *you*?" I ask.

"This is our Uncle Staran!" Kalia says, half through tears. "My dad's cousin! I thought you must have died on Keil!"

"I wish I had," Uncle Staran says. "I mean, I wished I had, until now."

"Excuse me." A woman detaches herself, hobbles toward us. I notice that her right hand ends at the wrist. Hollow-cheeked, hair falling out, but her eyes are alive, fierce. "I'm Paxin sher-Kohin. I'm a journalist. Are you with the Kurguls?"

"We were."

"Paxin sher-Kohin?" Scurv says. "We read your books, many years ago."

"Uh ... thank you," she says. "I didn't think anyone read those. Did you come ..." Her voice actually breaks. "Did you come to get us out of this place?"

I don't want to say I didn't figure on it. "What's going on here?"

"The Resistance put us here," Uncle Staran says, standing up and away from the kids. "The Chosen One himself, who I supported with my own money and my own vats! Who Paxin wrote about like he was some kind of hero! John Starfire corralled us, kept us penned like animals, and sent us all to die in an Imperial mine!"

"You en't prisoners?"

"Prisoners get cells," the one-handed woman, Paxin, says. "We sleep in the mines."

"We're all bluebloods, as you crosses like to say," Uncle Staran says. "The Resistance shipped us here to add to the workforce. A lot of the prisoners have been let go. We're moving out the oxygen cells three times the speed the original prisoners did."

"Because," Paxin interjects, "they were allowed to go back to their cells and sleep."

A woman near Uncle Staran touches Toq like he's some kind of thing she barely remembers. Her body more bones than meat. More miners are coming near us now. Dozens of them crowding us, with them skeletal faces, looking like they been starved for years.

"New shipments every week," Uncle Staran says. "New people coming in. All humans."

That would figure right with what the Resistance thinks of humans. "How many?"

"We're not sure. The word is that ten thousand have

come in. About a third of us have died already, from over-work, bad rations, and disease. I'm guessing that's constant."

Ten thousand bluebloods, right here in this mine. Ten thousand of them getting starved and worked to death. I feel so struck I en't able to do nothing but repeat it. "Ten thousand."

"More like seven thousand, with those who've died."

"Sense, it is," Scurv says. "Resistance wants the oxygen, wants the humans dead—John Starfire is an efficient man."

"Jaqi," Kalia says. "We have to rescue them! This is exactly what we're trying to stop!"

She's right, of course. This is the Reckoning right here, and these are the proof of John Starfire's own madness.

And our caper just went from stealing one prisoner back to stealing seven thousand of them.

———

Araskar

We drop into the maintenance tunnels, crouch, and run. Dull blue emergency lights play across Z's and X's tattooed skin. Z limps, running along the base of the tunnel. X clutches at the rip the Maata left across her thigh, but keeps going with me.

"Look for a weak panel!" I shout over the roar of the oxygen works.

"Will they send those guards after us?" X asks.

"They're all sick. And why send blobs after us when—"

The Maata presses its face against the small hole, and begins to slither through, its body compacting through the hole and then expanding again.

"Damn damn damn," I say.

"It still moves like a cat, save when it changes its shape," X says. "Interesting. Should it not be sick as well?"

"I guess the pathogen only affects certain types of fluids," I say. "The sentient ones. Not the big ugly, hungry ones."

The Maata flows into the tunnel, and re-forms, sleek, red eyes glowing in the dark, and its growl mingles with the roar of the oxygen works below us.

"We need to go below!" I yell over the sound, and I let go of Z, who slumps against the wall. I turn to confront the Maata, and realize I haven't got any weapons, except the shock stick's end that Z gave me. Probably burned out any residual charge.

The Maata growls and lashes out, and I feint backward—and its right paw becomes a tentacle, slithering like a snake along the wall to me. I jam the end of the shock stick into the tentacle.

It screams, shudders, and nearly loses shape, yanking the tentacle back.

That's good. A fluid sentient has a free-floating nervous system, more prone to disruptions of the electrical sort. If only I had an actual weapon.

I back up—and stumble into Z, who is punching out one of the metal panels on the side of the tunnel.

"That was brave. You might earn honor yet today," he shouts.

"How are you even standing?" I answer him. "That should have crippled you!"

"Honor makes me stand!" He furiously attacks the panel, and it screeches and screams, starting to lift off the rivets. "Honor makes me strong!" Wham. More hits and the metal pops off one rivet, revealing the roar and the green haze of the oxygen works below. The stink hits like a wall. "Go!" He seizes me and I yell "No!" but he tosses me through.

I go hurtling through the rank air, grab the first pipe I see, which breaks, shooting me with a blast of pure, heady oxygen. I go swinging out over the floor, crash into one of the big pillars, as it roars and shakes, sucking up oxygen cells.

Z's and X's voices are lost in the roar of the oxygen works all around me. Through the green haze, I see a large dark shape slipping between the pillars—the Maata.

Its sensory input will be as confused as ours, and this slick floor will do it no favors either. Of course, it's still bigger than both of us.

Another dark shape moves to my left, and I spin, armed with nothing but the shock stick point—

It's Rashiya's ghost.

"I'm lonely. Are you coming to me yet?"

"Not yet." Damn. I look back at the oxygen works, the particular centrifuge behind me. A roar and a *pop* echo through the works as one of the hyperdense cells is processed. I feel the suction on my legs, coming from the tiny open places at the bottom of the pillar.

"It's behind you," Rashiya says.

I ignore her and try to think back to what I learned on my oh-so-interesting tour. Hoppers of hyperdense cells under the floors. They move along at a regular click, and are sucked into the centrifuges inside the pillars, which break their integrity and then release enough oxygen to be pumped through all of Shadow Sun Seven. If only I had the shards, I could blow this whole place in two.

"I'm just telling you what your senses already tell you," Rashiya's ghost says, offhandedly.

I turn, and see two red eyes among the green haze.

It pounces, and I just move in time to avoid being gored by its horns, but not fast enough to avoid a claw. The claw catches my leg—the good part of my leg—and tears the flesh. I scream and tumble aside. The Maata should have me for dinner, but the slick floor works against it—it slides sideways, shifting its whole mass to try and deal with the change in weight. X comes out of the green mist and stabs the Maata in its side, her knife sinking in deep—and the Maata's side grows three sharp tentacles, lashing out at her. She tumbles away from it, lashes out with the makeshift whip of her sense-rope. Its side-tentacles grab the rope, yank it away.

I scramble to my feet, and nearly fall over from the pain. Stupid leg. I didn't have you reconstructed for nothing!

I hear another burst as a nearby centrifuge sucks up a hyperdense cell. Right next to me, the suction whirring through the same small grate where I dumped the pathogen on my tour.

Ignoring the intense pain of my leg, I kick the grate in. They're made to be just big enough for a regular sentient, in case a blob couldn't get in. "Hey! You!" I bellow.

"Me?" Rashiya's voice sounds next to my head.

"Not you, shut up!"

The Maata is still trying to get X, who has vanished behind another centrifuge. I jam the end of the shock stick into its rear.

It whirls around, every inch the enormous, hungry cat as it growls at me.

I look right into those red eyes and say, "I'm ready to die."

"Good boy," Rashiya says.

The Maata lunges, but it's still trying to maintain its footing, and the lunge falls short of me. I back up, and slip, fall on my back, and just manage to crabwalk backward to one of the centrifuge pillars. I mutter, "Please be stupid enough for this."

I scuttle through the grate, scraping my sides raw, and suddenly I'm below the massive centrifuge, inside the bottom of a huge open pillar. Above me, rings of air-processing circuitry stretch to the ceiling, all of them spinning slowly, in slightly different rotations from each other. I just avoid falling into the hole where I can see sprockets turning, bringing another hopper of hyperdense cells to be processed.

Here's where it'll happen.

The Maata presses itself against the opened grate, starts to ooze through. It smells my blood, no doubt.

From above me, Rashiya smiles down. "Is this it?"

"Might be," I say.

The Maata fills the space, roars at me, its red eyes

alight. Blood coats its teeth and claws. The Maata reaches for me—and the centrifuge above us whirls. Suddenly I start to lift off the ground. I hook my arm around a support strut. The Maata's shape changes as it tries to flatten out, cling to the slick, wet ground. It lashes long, furry tentacles onto various bits of the machinery, the grates—and from the hopper in the floor, hyperdense cells go sailing up, silver globules in the darkness. The Maata whines and tries to stretch out, but the suction is tougher on a fluid body than one with a bone structure like mine. It takes mental effort for a fluid sentient to maintain that shape.

One long tentacle loses a grip and is sucked up into the centrifuge. As one hyperdense cell explodes, the Maata screams and loses integrity to half its body; the rest starts to pull away, globs and globs of fluid-stuff spinning in the oxygen processor and being shot all over the station.

"Come on," Rashiya says. "Come to me."

My grip is slipping. The support strut is slick. And then the metal screams as someone tears it away, and the centrifuge screams louder, and all the Maata is gone and I can't cling any longer; I'm going to be sucked up hard enough to break all my bones and—

Two massive hands seize me under the shoulders, hold me in place as the centrifuge reaches its full status, and the Maata is completely discorporated, bits of cat and horns and claws becoming blue globules torn into pieces and spun with the exploding hyperdense cells.

Z's enormous tattooed arms link over my chest. My clothes tear. One of my boots flies off, up into the centrifuge.

And then it slows down, and bits of the Maata come down onto me in a warm sticky rain.

I don't think I'll ever hear again.

My ears are screaming in pain when Z pulls me out. Even so, I can tell what he mouths. *That was almost honorable.*

Thanks, asshole.

18

Jaqi

"ANY TROUBLE WITH THE GUARDS?" I ask the writer, as she leads us through the twisting tunnels of the mines, between hanging folds of flesh and hyperdense cells, all along the mag-tracks. The other miners are following us, for all that I en't sure that's such an idea. But if you're going to steal seven thousand people, might as well get them all there at once.

Seven thousand.

"The guards are all sick of a sudden," she says. "Your Kurguls took them by surprise, that's for sure. But more importantly, they can hardly hold their shape." Her eyes take in me and Scurv. "You can handle them."

Small comfort, that. "En't my Kurguls. I wouldn't admit to owning a one of them."

I can remember now, from the guard's memory, that he didn't think much on the mines. He didn't like it—remembered the miners as miserable, cold, skinny starved freaks. At the time, I didn't dwell much on that, as I was busy sifting his brainpan for information about the cell blocks.

I still feel a good bit of regret for that guard, I'm realizing a peculiar thing too—that guard, the fella didn't ask any questions, took his check and went. Just wanted to get home, to the kid.

Just like Swez said.

Took his check and went home.

It's what I used to do before them kids.

"If you can get us out of here—get us to a genuinely safe place—I know people who can get the word out," the writer says. She holds out the stump of her hand. "They wanted to stop me writing, but I promise you, I will write something every single sentient in the galaxy reads."

"Yeah, that's a fine idea," I say, not mentioning that I would not be able to read it. I start to walk, and Kalia shouts after me, "Jaqi, they can't walk very fast!"

The miners are fit to fall down and die, but they're crowding after us. Some of them are supporting others who are hurt. We pass others who have fallen, collapsed where they're standing. We pass some that obviously have gravity sickness—them are human types who spent their life on a real planet with real gravity, and these generators make them sick once they get old enough.

From where she's half holding her uncle up, Kalia says,

"Jaqi, what's our plan?"

"Our plan. Our plan." Okay, Jaqi, you en't no reader, but you still got the brainpan of a criminal. Use it like you en't used it before. "I reckon we can . . . I . . ." Aw hell. "I need to talk to Araskar." Cept he en't been answering again. <u>Slab, you there?</u>

Nothing.

And then, <u>Jaqi?</u>

<u>Slab, you're there!</u> <u>Thank all gods and Starfire. Look, where you at now?</u>

<u>The oxygen works.</u>

<u>I have a mighty problem, slab.</u>

<u>I——</u> He cuts off. A moment later. <u>I do too.</u>

I'm distracted as I notice smaller figures come out of the side tunnels to join us. "Children?" I say. "There are children in here?"

"Oh, yes," Paxin, the writer, says. "They can get into difficult places we cannot."

Burning Dark and shit in space. There's *kids,* too. "How long would it take to round up all of you?"

"Not too long," Paxin says. "Twelve hours?"

Twelve hours? Why not a week?

"What's our plan, Jaqi?" Kalia asks.

I look at Scurv. "Uh, slab, you got any ideas in your history?"

"I told you those comic books lie," Scurv says.

"Not what I need to hear, slab!"

"We say take the mission and leave, and return for the miners when there are greater advantages on our side." I must be giving vim the devil-eye, because vi holds vir hands up, as if to tell me to ease off. "You think there is some better solution, we are listening."

I can't leave this folk here. Not after killing a real innocent today, after seeing all the madness that the galaxy puts on folk. I need to get them all out of here.

Araskar speaks. <u>What's your problem? Did you get the prisoner?</u>

<u>Oh, we got the one. Problem is, it en't just the one.</u>

He don't answer that. I'm not sure what to say. I look around me, and my gaze takes in the rows and rows of folk, leaning on each other, leaning on the walls, even against the stacks of hyperdense cells.

Their eyes don't change. Faces are all thinned out from where they should be. Bodies like a Routalais; all thin, like skin's just fabric hung on bone. But their eyes are all the same. All hope.

Aw hell.

<u>You were saying?</u>

<u>Seven thousand people, slab. All like Kalia and Toq, bluebloods what was taken captive by the Resistance. We gotta get them home.</u>

Araskar don't answer right away, but I can figure what

he's thinking. <u>What does Swez say about that?</u>

<u>That's a problem too, slab. The Matakas are long gone.</u>
<u>Left us here.</u>

<u>Any ships?</u>

<u>Two barges.</u>

<u>Jaqi, we can't take all these people with us. I can't even</u>
<u>get back to my own shuttle.</u>

<u>We have to, slab! I won't let this happen! I won't let</u>
<u>this many innocents go down. We get them free, we</u>
<u>strike a blow against John Starfire. Innocent lives should</u>
<u>mean something in this damn galaxy!</u> I try to calm down,
but damn, this gets me riled. <u>I en't letting anyone else die.</u>

<u>Where the hell will we even take them?</u>

"Jaqi," Scurv says. "The loading dock."

The loading airlock gapes, a giant gap, with the stars
of space beyond the sense-field. The whole thing's been
cut into Shadow Sun Seven's side. Two of the automated
barges sit on the platform.

Them oxygen cells are everywhere. The Matakas may
have filled an entire barge-loader, but they left plenty of
wealth. All held together by bags of skin membrane, the
cells are piled in big old heaps everywhere you can guess.
A black metal platform rises out of the flesh, and there's
three barges parked along the platform. No place for a
loose shard.

And there is a ship coming into the airlock.

I've seen this kind of ship before, but it takes a long moment afore it clicks with me where I done seen it.

I shot one of these ships up at Bill's.

It's a Vanguard drop ship.

"Resistance troops. We've got . . ." I realize I've got one hand on the soulsword. Taltus's soulsword, the one is too big for me.

"A full squadron," Scurv says. Vi bites vir lip, and I reckon vi is calculating something in that cat-quick head of virs. "Forty, yes?"

"Forty."

"Forty is not too bad." Vi unholsters vir guns. "Remind me to kill the pilots, so the ship does not get away."

"Slab, one shard goes wrong and you'll blow every single person here away. We can't risk it. Maybe we can talk to them or—"

Scurv ignores me, walks up to the platform, and climbs the ladder.

Like a big damn fool, I follow vim. "Slab, you can't shoot here!"

We climb up over the lip of the platform to see a whole platoon of the Vanguard. Swords drawn, each one of them. I'm about ready to piss myself.

Their commander has the same face as that bearded fella I killed in Bill's. Same face as Araskar. Helmet is obscuring his face a bit, but there's a look I recognize in them eyes. The fella who stood over a six-year-old child, ready to kill him, and I clutch the soulsword, and I realize that no matter what happens, I en't backing down here.

"Surrender the children and the traitor Araskar."

"Out the airlock, assho—"

Scurv shoots him before I can finish my insult. A single green shard, flashing, hits that Vanguard scab right in the chest, blows his entire chest apart.

Before anyone can say a thing, Scurv shoots about ten more troops. Green shards flash, and then one's down, and then another, and then yet another, and one shoots a red shard that blasts apart the metal under Scurv—but Scurv moves, quick as a cat again, slipping to the side.

"No shooting!" one of them shouts. "One wrong shot, you blow this entire place! Soulswords!"

They whip out their swords, and some of them manage to deflect the shots that fly from Scurv's guns like air rushing out of a punctured ship. Green shards go flying, in a rush.

More hit flesh, tearing through armor, than hit soulswords.

"Don't fire back!" the troops yell—but I see others drawing sidearms, trying to save their lives—

And Scurv stops firing. And smiles.

"We were in prison a long time, sadly," vi says. "And our other selves"—vi cocks the guns—"need sustenance.

Not many shards left. Question we must ask now, is whether there are enough to take care of you all."

About fifteen soldiers remain, standing next to screaming, weeping, bleeding, and burned corpses. Vi's just taken out more than half the squad.

"Lucky, are we?"

"Grab a cell!" The remaining troops come for Scurv, swords drawn—and each of them rolling a hyperdense cell.

Scurv backs up a bit, till vi's at the edge of the platform—and smiles. Just like a cat at a mouse-hole.

"You don't dare shoot!" one of them yells. "You hit one of the cells, we all go up!"

"That would be the case," vi says. "If we ever missed."

And vi shoots.

Flash. One shard, across the way, one shard, in the midst of a million packed oxygen cells that could blow us all to hell—

It takes off a Vanguard head, neat as you please. Body and oxygen cell both fall.

Flash. Another shard. Another Vanguard head.

Flash. Again.

The troops get smart, hold the cells up in front of their faces, crouch down as they circle Scurv, suddenly reluctant.

Scurv gestures with vir gun. "Oh, we like this. Don't be too easy on us, aiya."

While I'm watching like some dumb cow, another soldier comes for me, soulsword raised. He yells some damn thing about the Resistance and John Starfire and nonsense, but all I can think is that I have accidentally drawn Taltus's sword, not the one Araskar gave me. It's about twice the size and weight of the one that fitted me before, and I wave it at him, trying not to drop the damn thing.

This bastard is fast. I back up, back up some more from him, and he keeps coming. Stabs and slashes, but I'm backing up faster than he can hit—until I back right up into the barge Swez left for me.

I swing the soulsword, but Taltus's blade is too heavy, and I lose my grip and it scrapes along the ground. I dodge just in time to keep the Vanguard soulsword out of my shoulder—and it sticks in the barge behind me. He grabs the short soulsword from his belt, stabs at me, but it turns on Taltus's blade, slices my side and my shirt.

I drop Taltus's sword and grab his neck with one arm, the short soulsword with the other, and we fall to the ground, wrestling for the short soulsword. The bastard is stronger than me, but I got a grip around his head, cutting off his air—and he's pushing the blade down, toward my chest, but I tighten my grip, lock it like Bill showed me, feel his neck compact under my grip—and the soulsword is through my shirt and poking into my skin—and he goes limp.

I stand up, gasp—and then throw myself down as one of Scurv's shards goes overhead.

I look up, my heart hammering. With each heartbeat, Scurv does the impossible.

One beat, vi shoots the feet off three Vanguard too busy covering their faces. They fall forward; vi shoots their heads. Neat as you please. No hyperdense cell touched.

Two, vi blows the heads off two Vanguard close enough trying to rush vir with their soulswords.

Three, couple others toss their oxygen cells at him, abandoning all sense. One-handed, the slab catches two oxygen cells and shoots the Vanguard with vir other hand.

Four, vi springs to the side, hits three of them—three—with two—two!—shards.

Five, vi jumps like a cat, lands behind two Vanguard, takes their heads off. Six—four Vanguard give up, draw their weapons, and vi shoots them all first, right over the weapons.

Seven, eight, nine—vi sends shards within a finger's width of them oxygen cells, blasts heads off shoulders, legs off waists—

Ten—they're *all* down—

A Resistance gauntlet grabs my arm, and I see the

soulsword flash, I jump away just in time, yanking my arm out of her grip, but now she's rushing me, yelling something indistinguishable about *you bastards you bastards.*

Scurv raises the pistol—then fires out the airlock. The shard bounces off the sense-field, rebounds, hits this Vanguard from *behind.*

I stumble away—and fall.

Scurv runs up the platform and there's more shooting from inside the Vanguard ship, and then vi walks out, across the metal platform to me. I stare up into the face of Scurv Silvershot, only sentient beside me alive in a sea of corpses.

Forty Vanguard.

Vi picks up a short soulsword, tosses it in the air, and just to scare the hell out of me, shoots it. It glows white-hot and goes spinning across the platform, within a few feet of the cells.

"Damn it, don't play!"

"We cannot resist a little flash," Scurv says.

I can't even be mad. "Them comics don't lie," I say.

"They lie plenty," vi says. "Just not about the shooting."

Araskar

I gasp for air, feeling my body, on the floor of the swampy chamber, my whole body wet with sweat and condensation. Not dead yet. Not dead yet.

Of all times, now I notice that it sounds almost comforting not to be dead.

"Araskar," Z says.

"What now?" I try to get up. My arms feel as worn out as old rope.

"Both you and Xeleuki-an-Thrrrrr-Xr-Zxas have shed blood this day. I should be more crippled than both of you but I feel hale, all pain and shaking gone from my limbs in the decisive moment of battle. I—have the ancestors made me immortal?"

"Jaqi did a miracle," I say, staggering to my feet. "Don't question it too hard."

"The ancestors have truly sent you back for a reason," X says.

"They have sent me back to kill the Faceless Butcher—"

"To finish this mission!" I groan.

X gets to her feet as well. "Come, Zarag-a-Trrrro-Rr-Zxz. The battle is not over. The Faceless Butcher must yet die today. I feel the ancestors singing, waiting for us at the River of Stars. They know for what we fight."

"Yes. We will return to the pit, and call for him."

"Will you shut up about that?" I say.

"Indeed, he—agh!"

X twists, but not enough. The bone-headed spear enters her body, emerges bloody from below her right breast.

She roars, louder even than the oxygen works. Roars, and she forces her body down and breaks the shaft of the spear. Blood and viscera flow from her and she spins, mortally wounded but quick still.

The NecroSentry emerges from the mists, holding my soulswords, the bastard. "Death," he roars. "Finally, death!"

X is not done, though. She lunges for him. He brings up the soulsword, drives it into her chest. She digs her claws into the eyehole of his helmet, and he bellows, and shoves her against the nearest pillar, cutting with the soulsword, but she triumphantly tears an eye from his head and holds it aloft.

He screams, yanks out the sword from his chest. X slides, bloody, along the pillar, still holding aloft the NecroSentry's severed eye.

Not another useless death. Damn it.

Z pulls me to my feet, and puts me behind him. Those black claws come out of the ends of his fingers again. He bellows at the NecroSentry, "I have cheated death! Will you fight me, then, when I have best your master? I have made a mockery of death, and returned!"

The NecroSentry rushes him—and loses its balance, flailing, and dropping one of my soulswords.

My sword goes sliding along the ground of the oxygen works. My sword at last. I dive for it, roll along the wet ground, come up holding it—

And see several dozen other soulswords glowing in the darkness. Coming for me.

Jaqi?

Slab, you're there! I can hear the relief in her voice. Thank all gods and Starfire. Look, where you at now?

The oxygen works.

I have a mighty problem, slab.

I— Three Resistance soldiers run out of the haze, brandishing blades and running for me. I do too.

I back up.

The word *traitor* forms on their lips.

Word's gotten out.

They slow when they realize how slick the floor is. One, braver than the others, attacks me. I parry her blows, and slide on the floor, trying to catch every blow and turn them away from me. Not easy, when I'm trying not to slip, and my whole body's screaming from the beating it got just this morning—oh, and the hours I spent drugged and crammed into a locker.

<u>What's your problem now, slab?</u>

Our swords clatter, spraying moisture droplets. I back up and nearly slip; catch myself just in time to block a thrust from my opponent. I've been backed against the pillar where X lies bleeding out, staring, the floor even slicker than usual with her blood.

<u>Did you get the prisoner?</u>

<u>Oh, we got the one. Problem is, it en't just the one.</u>

"Araskar!" the soldier fighting me shouts. "Don't resist, traitor! Don't resist!"

"Don't resist," Rashiya's ghost says.

The Vanguard soldier rushes me, putting too much weight into her thrust.

And X, in one last gesture, whips that sense-rope, the coil bright white around my opponent's leg, yanks her off-balance. My opponent loses balance and my sword goes right through her middle.

I kick the Resistance soldier away. With one bloody hand X presses the sense-rope into mine.

"I'm sorry," I say.

"My honor." She smiles, mouthing the words, unable to speak with ruined lungs. "I have gained my honor back."

"We'll sing of you. I hope there are ancestors waiting for you, X."

"Of course there are." She dies with a smile on her face.

I shove the sense-rope into my belt. Another one of the Resistance runs for me, holding her blade more cautiously. Her opponent flanks me. Trying to back me into a corner, but they'll still have a hell of a time killing me with a couple of swords.

And that's when Z and the NecroSentry, a massive, roiling, bloody wrestling pair, slide right into the first Resistance soldier and throw her against a pillar. The NecroSentry angrily seizes her by the arm and tosses her at Z. He ducks and she bounces off a pillar.

Seven thousand people, Jaqi says.

The other Resistance soldier charges me and I lose the thread of what Jaqi was saying. I back up some more, and my back hits another pillar, rumbling with oxygen processing. I catch his blade, and I see fear in his eyes. He's got the same face as me, but unscarred, perfect. I press my attack, despite the way his sword cuts into my leg. It catches, half a second, on the synthskin and his eyes widen and he realizes he's dead and—

I jam my sword through his solar plexus.

But I can't stand to have any more ghosts haunting me, no matter how useful the memories might be. I don't take the memories.

He writhes on the ground, choking on his blood.

Still not dead yet.

Z roars something from the depths of the oxygen

works. There'll be another Resistance soldier after me soon enough. More soulswords glow in the distance, near that elevator. You were saying?

Seven thousand people, slab. All like Kalia and Toq, bluebloods what was taken captive by the Resistance. We gotta get them home.

Well, shit. What does Swez say about that?

That's a problem too, slab. The Matakas are long gone. Left us here.

Shit, shit, shit. Any ships?

Two barges.

Two barges. Maybe two hundred people could fit all told? Not a patch on seven thousand. Hell, damn and burning Dark. Jaqi, we can't take all these people with us. I can't even get back to my own shuttle.

We have to, slab! I won't let this happen! I won't let this many innocents go down. We get them free, we strike a blow against John Starfire. Innocent lives should mean something in this damn galaxy! I en't letting anyone else die here!

Where the hell will we even take them?

I bend over the dead Vanguard soldier.

He's still gagging on his blood. His eyes, the exact same color and shape as mine, stare up at me. Will I look that afraid when I finally die?

I force myself to look down at his bloodstained chest.

I guarantee these troops were briefed not to bring shards into the oxygen works, or anywhere near the hyperdense cells. Guarantee it.

I also guarantee you this: no soldier will ever give up a sidearm, not unless they've lost their mind. Even when the sidearm could get them killed. And I guarantee you that whoever drew "look-for-Araskar-in-oxygen-works" duty didn't bother checking their soldiers for sidearms.

I feel around his belt.

Yeah, he's carrying a small shard-blaster, the kind of thing you stick in the back of your waist pocket. I yank it out, get plenty of his blood and sweat on my hand. The shards inside glow red.

A live gun.

All it will take is a couple of shots, and we'll be rid of this entire oxygen works.

And ourselves. And half of Shadow Sun Seven.

Z runs to me. "Come!" He seizes me by the arm, and we run across the wet floor, slipping and sliding.

The one eye of the NecroSentry glares through the green mists behind us. He's closing on us.

Z yanks open a door in the wall, and shoves me inside. I fall over onto a pile of hyperdense cells, stumbling, trying not to plunge the hand holding the shard-blaster into the hyperdense cells and blow us all up. I stumble, and for one second the glowing red shard-blaster hovers above the bright orb of a cell and I am about to tip over onto it—and I get my balance.

I stand there heaving with relief. "Damn it, Z!"

"There are more Vanguard troops coming in," he says. "I think the Faceless Butcher discovered your identity."

"Yeah, I caught that."

Slab? You there?

The NecroSentry pounds on the door, and the mag-locks screech. Z nearly bounces away from the door. "I must go battle the NecroSentry," he groans. "Though there is no honor in fighting a thing that was already dead, I think there is honor in avenging Xeleuki-an-Thrrrrr-Xr-Zxas, who sold her life bravely in the name of killing the Faceless Butcher."

"Glad you figured that out."

Araskar, you en't lost that sword again? Where are you?

Hang on, I tell Jaqi. Something the Boss said comes back to me, as I look down from the hanging slab of dead Zarra across the pile of hyperdense cells . . . and down to the glowing shard-blaster in my hand.

Boss Cross's words. If we have any problems, this is where the mines will separate from the, ah, head.

This is crazy. I should just go out there and sell my life as dearly as I can.

"You should come to me," Rashiya's ghost says.

Well, when she says it I don't want to do it.

Jaqi, I say. I have the craziest plan in history. We're going to split off the mines from the rest of the prison. You just rig something up to drag the bug's bottom end to the node.

Hang on, slab, I'm getting shot at.

"Z," I say, and raise the pistol I took off the Resistance soldier. "I have a question for you about honor."

"Now is not—urg—" The pounding on the door knocks him away from it, but he returns to his post. "An ideal time."

"Is there honor in laying explosives?"

The door crashes open. The NecroSentry looms above us.

I shoot the NecroSentry.

The shard takes most of his head and shoulders off, but his arms remain, flailing around on a headless torso. Thankfully, his bulk also absorbs the whole of the shard—no red fragments go flying, and so we aren't prematurely blown to hell.

"You have robbed me of honor!" Z snarls, as he rears up and kicks the flailing corpse away. "An' you could have blown this entire place up!"

I check the load. A few more shards in this gun. "That's the idea. How do you feel about a really big explosion?"

Z thinks for a minute, then says, "They are honorable, under the right circumstances."

"Oh good. I would hate to have the wrong circumstances for that."

-19-

Jaqi

SCURV AND I KICK the bodies of the Resistance soldiers off the platform. Vi does that business again where vi bites vir lip and examines the ship. "This will fit forty people," vi says, and motions beyond the platform, where the miners are massing. "Forty. Them barge will fit another hundred and sixty."

It's been a while since I seen this many folk in one place. Forty people seems like a tall order. But there's at least a couple of thousand out there, having put down their mining gear with the blobs' sickness.

"I en't taking just forty," I tell Scurv. "I'm taking them all."

Vi doesn't answer me.

I'm taking a full seven thousand, damn it. I grab the soulsword's hilt. <u>What's that you said about the craziest plan in history?</u> I ask Araskar. <u>Slab, you there?</u> I think, before I realize that this en't the cross sword I'm holding, but Taltus's much larger blade.

And a voice bellows into my head, like it's about to pop open.

ADEPT TALTUS. YOU HAVE CALLED UPON THE SACRED VORTEX OF FAITH. EXPLAIN YOUR NEED.

Uh . . . Hell, am I hearing the voice of God? This en't Taltus. This is Jaqi.

JAQI. YOU ARE AN ADEPT? WHY DO YOU BEAR THE BLADE OF TALTUS? HOW CAN YOU SPEAK THROUGH IT? NONE BUT AN ADEPT OF THE MASKED FAITH CAN SPEAK THROUGH THE BLADE.

En't no Adept. En't nothing. Taltus gave me the blade, when he died. What's this business about faith?

THE BLADE WAS NEVER HIS TO GIVE AWAY. YOU MUST RETURN THE BLADE. AN ADEPT'S BLADE IS SACRED.

Taltus never told me his blade could connect to his elders. Without even a node-relay?

Unless I'm having some sort of effect on it. How can you even hear me? I'm on the other side of the galaxy.

YOU ARE NOT IN-SYSTEM? HOW ARE YOU SPEAKING TO US?

Okay, well it en't the blade. I hold up the sword and stare at it. What the hell? I always been good with nodes, and we can't be more than three miles out from Shadow

Sun Seven's node—but damn, really?

I am pushing this message through a node?

Almost a miracle, that.

<u>HOW ARE YOU DOING THIS?</u>

Good question. <u>Hang on—</u> Who better than a bunch of religious types to take in seven thousand refugees? Maybe they'd weasel out of it if I asked, but if I can turn up on their doorstep. <u>I'm coming, uh, with the blade. Where you at?</u>

<u>FOR ADEPT TALTUS'S SAKE, YOU COULD MEET WITH ANY ONE OF OUR REPRESENTATIVES—</u>

<u>Naw, slabs, I'll come to you. Just tell me where. Thuzerians still running out of the Llyrixan system?</u>

<u>YES.</u>

<u>I'll be right there. Won't take but a minute out of my schedule to get you this sword.</u>

As plans go, this one en't exactly high-grade. But it'll get the refugees in front of a bunch of religious types, and they'll be able to take those folk in, at least for a while. Right? No one like religious types to take in the poor and sick.

I don't know. Hell, I never smuggled living cargo. I'm making this business up as best I can.

I grab the other soulsword. <u>What's this about the craziest plan ever? Reckon I found a place of peace we can take these folk.</u>

There's Araskar. <u>Can you rig up some way to tow the mines to the node?</u>

<u>Tow them? Tow all of Shadow Sun Seven to the node?</u>

<u>Not all of it.</u> A mental picture slams into my head from Araskar, nearly knocks me over with the pounding pain. Oxygen works, making a sort of neck for this creature. If there's an accident in the volatile oxygen works, both halves of Shadow Sun Seven are programmed to separate.

<u>We'll separate the mines. The oxygen should last long enough to get to the node, if you can rig up a decent tow. Tug the bottom half of the bug.</u>

I see what he's saying. A mad plan, but . . . I look over at Scurv, chewing vir lip. "Aiya, slab. You reckon you can rig up this drop ship to tow this place?"

"Tow the entire prison? We are not sure we heard you right."

"We're going to try and break the bit with the mines off."

"This seems like a good way to destroy us all."

"It's meant to separate. Like that holo when you was on that ship and they separate the bit at the top from the bottom because them Suits are attacking—en't you familiar with this?"

Scurv laughs, idly pets one of vir guns. "That never truly happened, girl." Vi points behind the platform, at the mines. "There will be tow ropes in the drop ship, and we could hook them around the endoskeletal struts. We will not be able to build up much speed, but we can try towing."

"Don't matter," I say. "Just get us there."

Vi walks up the platform into the drop ship, and returns with rope. "This is one of the madder things we have done, in our time."

"It'll make a good comic book."

———————

Araskar

I pull aside the hyperdense cells—one at a time, very carefully—until I see the controls for the old hopper under the floor. "Here we are."

"You found it?" The soldiers hammer against the door, Z bracing himself, shoving his shoulders against the metal. He's shoved the remaining meat of the NecroSentry against the door, in order to help block it. On the other side, what sounds like at least five Resistance troops pound the door.

The NecroSentry's not-quite-dead arms feel around, like they're trying to grab weapons. Z kicks the corpse. "Stay down," he hisses. "You should have allowed me to finish this thing, for Xeleuki-an-Thrrrrr-Xr-Zxas."

"Not enough honor," I say. I run my fingers over the controls. "Needed to save you for something really great. Like I thought. This room's a backup in case the main feeds fail. Pretty easy to turn on."

Z leaps aside as the point of a soulsword jabs through the metal. He whacks the soulsword's blazing tip with the NecroSentry's knife, trying to bend it before it's jerked back through the door.

I cinch X's sense-rope around the lip of a wide, flat rivet set into the floor. "I turn on the track that carries this hopper, and then I'm going to see what happens when I overload the system with oxygen and shards. If I'm right, we have an explosion like a Shir fart, and Shadow Sun Seven splits in two."

"And I am going to fight all these soldiers while you do that." Two more soulswords cut through the metal of the door.

"I don't want to be the only one who goes out in a blaze of glory," I say.

"Glory and honor are two different things."

"Hate to say it, but I don't think you'll ever get to explain the distinction to me."

"I am aware of this. It saddens me."

"You know," I say as I drop into the little metal tunnel, "Jaqi made you promise to stay alive."

"She does not understand what a difficult request this is."

"We might survive this." I don't know why I'm suddenly so optimistic, but I want to hope. "If John Starfire can lead an army of scrappy crosses to victory over the Empire, then we might come out of this one alive, and fight another day."

"It is foolish to ask such things." The door is being cut to ribbons now, the white light of the soulswords shining through. "Also, foolish to invoke your enemy's success to guide your own. But if the ancestors choose to send me back again, I will find you, Araskar."

"And apologize for stuffing me into a locker?"

"And insist I was right about the Faceless Butcher."

Zarra. "Don't let them get into this tunnel," I say.

"My honor on it."

I grab several of the medium-sized hyperdense cells and, one at a time, feed them into the hopper on the tunnel.

I turn it on and the hopper starts to move. I drop onto the track behind it, crouch in the tunnel. The track moves me along under the floor. It's tight enough that I'm hunched over, back scraping against the ceiling. With my soulsword, I breach the chamber of the gun—just enough. All you need is a crack in the gun's housing, showing through to the shard-chamber. I toss it in the hopper, already stuffed full of hyperdense shards.

I've cracked a lot of pistols to create makeshift grenades. It should hold out until it hits the centrifuge. I hope.

Then again, either way it'll blow me mostly to hell.

The track pulls me until the rope around my waist goes taut, and I scramble backward against the track, crab-walking until I reach a small alcove, sized for the Reveks who do maintenance in here. It's too small for me, but I duck into the alcove and when another hopper comes by, I grab it, wrench it off the track, hold it against the alcove, pressing myself into the corner.

And I immediately feel stupid. Why am I trying to preserve my life? What do I have to live for? This is it.

Finally dead.

Rashiya's ghost whispers in my ear. "I knew you wanted to be with me."

I find myself thinking of Jaqi. Of her on the moon of Trace. *Hope you danced.* And I actually smile. I want to see her again. I want to watch her go on about food. I want to learn to play that stupid guitar.

Life is funny.

Nothing is easier, and none of my friends are alive. But when you get right down to it, there are things worth living for even in a lousy life. And though she won't want to hear it, I feel like I learned that from Jaqi.

The world lights on fire.

———————

Jaqi

The drop ship is all hooked up, heavy cable normally used to moor the ship in emergencies. Scurv is sitting in the cockpit, figuring vi will be a better shot with the limited weapons on board than I would.

All right, slab, I say to Araskar for the fifth time. All right—

The explosion knocks me to the ground, tosses the miners everywhere. The drop ship trembles, pushes against its spurs, nearly tumbles off the platform, but Scurv fires the engines and the ropes go taut.

The lights flicker and go out, leaving us standing in the red light of the drop ship's engines, the only illumination in the mines. The air tastes of smoke and cold, and my chest hurts—the oxygen is escaping.

Also, I feel about thirty pounds lighter. It'll take a while, but the grav-field en't pumping out no more, so unless we can spin this thing up on our own, we're going to start floating.

It worked, Jaqi.

Slab?

Araskar doesn't answer.

"Kalia!" She's standing next to me, along with that half-starved, one-handed reporter. "The air is gonna leak. We need to tap some of them cells." I look at the reporter. "You got any equipment to do a tap?"

"Maybe," she says. "The guards might know. Sometimes, if the oxygen quality is poor in the mines, we find small cells—about the size of your head—and detonate them."

"That'll have to do," I say. "Let's get looking for small cells that can be broken without too much fuss."

Oxygen rushes past me, out the airlock. Kalia and I paw through the piles of hyperdense cells looking for pieces small enough to detonate. "Jaqi, here's—" Kalia coughs and hacks as she hands me a cell the size of my forearm.

"Stand on back," I say, and jab the cell with Taltus's sword.

The explosion knocks me onto my back, whacks my head hard enough that I see stars. But there's sweet, sweet air. I stumble to my feet, hand the sword to Kalia. "Do a few more."

"Okay," she says. "Okay, Jaqi, okay—I'm scared—"

"Shh." I put a hand on her shoulder. "We won. You en't got nothing to worry about. We w—"

That's when the shards flash outside.

They pass just off Scurv's bow, and vi fires a few times—and I look up to see the large Vanguard warship. Just like the one Araskar rode around in.

Sitting right between us and the node.

"What are they doing?" Kalia says. "They won't fire on us—"

They fire again.

Scurv twists the drop ship to take the hit. The shards blow apart on the drop-ship's sense-field, toss it to the side, and tear off an antenna that isn't covered by the field. The chunk of antenna glowing hot metal, crashes into the platform and embeds itself into the barges still parked there, barely missing the hyperdense cells. The cells fly everywhere in the low gravity, bouncing off the walls.

I think I pissed myself.

Scurv's voice comes over the comm I'm still wearing. "That is it for our shields. Next shot we catch for you, girl, this drop ship will break apart."

"They won't shoot," Kalia says. "They'll destroy the stores of oxygen."

"I reckon, girl, that the Resistance cares less about that oxygen than about killing us." I hardly realize I'm saying them words.

"They won't kill us all!" Kalia says. "All these people!

All these—bluebloods."

Shit.

She embraces me, of a sudden, whispers, "Thank you, Jaqi. You tried."

I look up at the Vanguard ship. *No, damn it. We won. We won!*

We need a miracle.

20

Araskar

FIRE ROARS THROUGH THE tunnel; I'm jerked backward, the pain overtakes me as my skin burns, I pass out for the moment.

And then—

The cold awakens me; the cold every soldier fears; that cold of thin, evaporating atmos as space steals in. And though the cold awakens me, I can't move. Pain comes with it. Not dead yet, but burned, bloody, possibly broken.

No. I wanted this to be fast, damn it. Not slow asphyxiation and freezing.

"You shouldn't have protected yourself," Rashiya's ghost says.

I didn't want to die, I try to say, but there is no air in my seared lungs—and then the metal hiding me from the Resistance soldiers tears away, and a half-burned monster seizes me, pulls me out of the hole where I'm hiding.

The monster looks weirdly like Z, if Z had most of his

skin burned off. The horns are right, anyway. And as I watch, as the monster pulls me out of my hole and goes, hand-over-hand, along what used to be the floor, through the near-vacuum, that skin begins to reassemble itself, healing from the raw, bloody burned state.

My eyes must be fooling me. It makes sense, since the moisture in my eyes is freezing from the vacuum—

Z shoves me down a tunnel. I tumble through dodgy gravity, bouncing off the walls of the Threg's guts. Sweet oxygen rushes over me. I take an icy breath, gasp and suck in what little oxygen remains, as it's being also sucked out into space.

"Z—" I try to say the words, but my tongue is too numb, my body in too much pain.

"So close to the end now," Rashiya's ghost says. She's dead, all gray like she was when I buried her, a corpse without breath or memory, under one shovelful after another of dirt. "So close to me. You don't want to live now, do you?"

She says it, but I think I'm alive. I think this worked. I reach, with a hand that unclenches painfully, for the hilt of my soulsword. <u>Jaqi, it worked.</u>

I want her to hear me. I want someone besides these ghosts to hear me.

"She can't hear you," Rashiya's ghost says. "It's okay. You can die now. You can finally die! Why don't you want to die?"

I blink, because something strange is happening in the actual world. Z, the strangely healing-before-my-eyes Z, deposits me in the tunnel, turns around, and jumps out into the vacuum.

Or he tries to jump. He kind of stumbles, trips, and floats, trying to push off against the still-remaining residual gravity. Whatever's happened to him, it's taken the energy out of him. He feebly swims, a pale figure against an ocean of stars and debris. Like he's trying to reach Shadow Sun Seven's head, spinning off into the distance, shedding debris.

What the hell?

Despite the pain, somehow I manage to move. Manage to loop the broken rope that is still attached to my waist around the endoskeletal spur that runs through this section of mines. Manage to tie it, burned fingers fumbling.

I leap out into space for Z. He sees me, and although he can barely move, gagging on his words, there is still fury in his eyes.

No air left to answer him. It is biting cold, a cold that rips into me, that frosts over the burns and cuts on my skin. It is silent, empty, nothing but the stars, the drifting debris and us. My body aches from the lack of air, from the moisture freezing inside me. But I am still a cross. The data dump told us we could survive a full two minutes in vacuum. If I am fast enough.

I grab Z with one arm, hook it under his armpit, and begin pulling us back along the rope. Whatever strength possessed him a moment ago has been used up, seemingly by his rapid healing, however that works.

I pull, and we move slowly, a thread in the airless darkness. I pull, trying to ignore the way my hands feel distant from me, and the way my whole body's become a numb, cold block, pull us back toward the mines.

"You're coming to me after all," Rashiya's ghost says.

The spit freezes painfully on my tongue, as I speak unheard words. "The hallucinations should stop now. The pathogen can't survive out here."

Her hand slides, a thin trembling cold sensation, up my arm. "I said I'd be with you to the end. What makes you think I'm a hallucination?"

"Because," I say, soundlessly, "I don't want to die."

I pull, one pull at a time, until we are back in the thin atmos of the mines.

Jaqi

I speak on the comm. "Scurv, you got any shots left?"

"The ship's blaster is damaged."

"Can you climb out and take a few shots?"

Scurv's cold voice in my ear. "We are not miracle workers. And we are out of shards besides. Our other selves need to eat to make more."

Araskar's voice intrudes. Jaqi, I'm here. I have Z.

I en't got the heart to tell him.

We just got to get to that node. It en't but a few miles out, by Imperial reckoning. A quick flight on thrusters.

Back on Swiney Niney, when we was getting chased by the gray girl, Araskar's pal, I made my shard-shots count. I just looked at her and I reckoned she was like a node—but that only worked on crosses, and I en't sure them gunships are populated by crosses.

Just got to get to that node.

Hang on.

I sent a message through the node without even trying. And I could find a node if you dropped me on the wildest wild world. Got an evil sense for that. Don't no one know how to make new nodes—hell, I know plenty of folk have died trying—but maybe I can *move* one.

It's only a few miles. Hardly a peck of distance in space.

I reach out. We're close enough I can feel the node. I en't got the words to explain how it feels, but it's just *there* for me. Nodes've always been that way for me. Like they's standing there waving just for Jaqi, even though for most sentients they en't nothing but an invisible spot in the darkness, a spot you can only open by transmitting the right code on a pure-space frequency. But I never needed no codes.

I reach out for the node. Normally, I wouldn't try reaching when I'm this far out—I know there's no way to get the ship to the node that way.

I try to touch it, to reach it the way I would to throw my ship into it. Come on.

Kalia clings to me, crying softly, as the air streams out of here and our lungs ache. Come on.

Come on, now. The node is fixed to one place in real space, and a different spot in pure space, and we can go through pure space instantaneously, and I just need to take us through to the Llyrixan node, which I been through plenty of times, the Thuzerians not being proof against the occasional catch of illegal matter.

Fixed to one spot in real space. I just need to change that spot. I can feel the node, but it's far away, and my grip is weak.

The shards erupt from the Vanguard ship. We are all washed in red light.

Come on. Come one. No more Bills. No more Quinns. No more folk dead for the wrong reasons.

And as weak as my grasp is, I *grab* that node, and

somehow, like I'm unspooling a string I didn't know was there, I bring it to us and—

Everything goes white.

21

Araskar

IT'S THE MOST WRENCHING trip I've ever had through pure space. Despite what they tell you about crosses, this gets my stomach. All the thurkuk secretion and booze comes up right onto Z's freshly restored, smooth, and un-marked face.

Once my vision restores itself, coalesces outside of the distortion of pure space, I see an un-tattooed Zarra covered in my vomit, huddled against the wall of this tunnel into the mines

He has a whole new frown for this.

More to the point, there's a beautiful blue and green planet below us. Land and water and all the things there are to love about a planet.

"What has been done?" Z gapes, his voice thin and faint in the leaking atmos.

Right as if on cue, a massive Thuzerian dreadnought soars overhead. The ship throws us into shadow, a solid asteroid-sized troop carrier.

Words reverberate through me.

I can't say how I feel the message—they must be talking to Jaqi, because it echoes through my sense of her, like the words float on a torrent of her music.

<u>WHAT IS THIS?</u>

Jaqi doesn't answer.

I wonder if they'll hear me. With my bloody, burned hand, I clench my soulsword's hilt and say, <u>Refugees seeking asylum.</u>

<u>WHAT REFUGEES?</u>

<u>The Reckoning. With seven thousand refugees from John Starfire's purges. Will you take us in, or let us die here?</u>

A moment, apparently while they're thinking through the galactic ramifications of this. And finally they say, <u>YOU BROUGHT THE WAR WITH YOU.</u>

<u>The war finds you.</u>

Nothing like military monks for efficiency, it turns out. The stories of the Thuzerians are true—they make the Imperial Navy look like a bunch of slow morons. It explains why both the Empire and Resistance were so eager to get the help of these fellows.

The Thuzerians, luckily, have an enormous ship's bay.

That said, there's still not enough room for all the refugees onboard their ship, and instead, they send technicians to cover the hind end of Shadow Sun Seven with a much more durable field that will retain oxygen, and they pump warm air into the field while they load people into a more human situation.

So while the miners are stuck in the mines for a while, no one's going to freeze and suffocate in vacuum.

More dreadnoughts come out of space, returning from deeper-orbit patrol, to help off-load refugees.

They patch me up as much as I can. I'm covered in severe burns, but all my moving parts still move, and the cold of space seems to have helped with the shock, along with my normal cross stamina.

I can't yell at Jaqi for not thinking this through, as she won't wake no matter how much we shake her and shout at her. She lies splayed out on the platform of what was Shadow Sun Seven's loading port.

That's two miracles for her.

For lack of Jaqi, soon enough I'm standing on the bridge of this dreadnought, trembling, well aware of the raw bloody burns all over my body.

And still smelling a bit of vomit. They did clean me up, but they had a lot of people to deal with.

A few refugees were too frail to survive the journey through pure space, but otherwise we don't have any casualties. The blobs have all surrendered in exchange for inoculation against the pathogen.

In a matter of hours, the first batch of refugees will be transported to the planet below, at the same time the last and hardiest of the refugees are being taken from the barges.

It's over.

And here I stand, in the lift to the bridge of this ship. Z is with me, as is Kalia, although Jaqi has been taken to the medical bay, since she won't wake up.

I don't know where this one we did the whole mission for—Scurv Silvershot—really? The real one?—has vanished to. For all I know, Scurv stole a ship and is already out of here. Great.

Z is eating. Since we got in the lift, he's consumed five protein packs. The kind that last most sentients a week each. His now-un-tattooed face is stained with crumbs of protein. Around the smacks of rapid chewing, he says, "You should not have taken me back."

"I saved your damn life."

"No, you robbed me of my honor. Now I will be forced to kill you."

Of course. "Give it some time, would you?" I ask.

"I will allow you to return to your full strength. Then I will kill you."

The doors to the lift open and we're on the Thuzerians' bridge.

I stand on the bridge, facing a whole bunch of very big sentients. Thuzerians seem to attract big types. A couple of Sska, like Taltus, but shorter. The captain could be human, but she's twice as big as any human I've met, and she has four arms, so she must be some sort of cross. Her mask is much more ornamental than Taltus's was, inscribed with scrollwork, covering only most of her nose.

Besides the masks, they all wear armor. I know it's overlapping synthsteel, but over it they wear tabards of white and red, with the symbol of a flaming soulsword printed on the fabric, and each of them has a black-bladed, hand-forged soulsword at the waist.

"What have you done?" she asks me, right off.

"Refugees," I say, my voice scratching.

"I know they're refugees," she says. "But they are also political prisoners. We're taking names as they're processed—these are all people the Resistance has disappeared over the last few months. Imperial families. Voting seats on multi-system Councils. Bluebloods, as the godless would call them." She raises an eyebrow. "Why do you have seven thousand of the Empire's most valuable citizens? Not to mention journalists!"

"What do you call them?" I think I might fall over. "If not bluebloods?"

"Now, we call them the hungry, poor, the tired, and the

wretched." I recognize the quote from the Bible.

"Welcome in the arms of the Lord," Kalia says.

"They shall inherit the stars."

"Good. Lovely." I am really going to fall over. "Can I sit down?"

She leads us into a council chamber, just to the right of the bridge, where I nearly collapse into a chair much too nice for my vomit-covered cross self. Z and Kalia sink into the chairs as well.

Despite the fact that I saw Z covered in burns, he's fine. He's got his skin back. His fingers and legs all work. But his tattoos, like I said, are gone—he's nothing but ice-white skin. It seems Jaqi not only healed him for time, but forever.

He's still eating, too. Six protein packs now. My forty-man regiment went through six a week.

"Taking you in—this will be seen as a political act, no matter how we spin it." She hesitates. "We have taken other prisoners before. Other refugees."

"Other humans?" I ask.

"Some humans," she answers carefully.

"The kinds of humans the Resistance might want to kill?"

"In the Lord, all are made new. We don't ask questions of the refugees who come to our door." She exhales. "But now, we cannot help but find out who we are taking in, when there are seven thousand coming at once."

I lean forward. "Do you know who I am?"

"Your face is certainly familiar. I fought against the Imperial Navy, when I was younger, and killed many with that face."

I like that she can say this without any disturbance. My kind of woman. "Captain."

"Adept. Adept Alsethus." She is a hard-looking woman, and I believe she's seen plenty of action in her time.

"Adept Alsethus. If you've paid any attention to the hits the Resistance puts out, probably the biggest one is for me. John Starfire wants my head on a pike. Look familiar now?"

"We do not have any contact with the Resistance," Alsethus says. "That said, I believe you."

"Good. Glad you believe me. John Starfire issued an order, one only the highest levels of his troops know—Vanguard. It's called Directive Zero." It's actually hard to talk about this. "You know the Three Directives of the Resistance."

"Justice for the fallen, recognition for the living, equity for the unborn." She nods, that ornate mask going up and down. "I am familiar with the Resistance."

"Directive Zero is an order to kill all humans." I can't help smiling. "Less poetic."

"Not all humans," she says. "Just those you call blue-bloods, surely."

"All humans. Every single one. And to give himself time to conduct this, John Starfire made a deal with the Shir." She flinches, and makes a sign against evil. "He promised the Shir that they could take the wild worlds to satiate their hunger."

"They'll only multiply, and increase the Dark Zone." Alsethus pauses a moment, and mutters something. I recognize this, the same way I recognized Kurgul, information filtering in from my data dump. It's a prayer in a dead language. *Oh God, hold back the great spiders.* "These are monstrous accusations. You tell me the hero of the galaxy is in league with Belial itself?"

"I'm sure you've heard worse accusations leveled against John Starfire," I say. "The universe doesn't lack for conspiracies. But you believe me."

"I have some cause to."

I'm going to tell her more. I'm going to tell her that I killed Rashiya, and I took the memories that came with Rashiya's death, and I know John Starfire's sins in and out, but Z interrupts me. "We have a girl with us. She is the Son of Stars."

"What?" Alsethus says.

Z stands up, looking weirdly naked without those tattoos, and brushes a few crumbs of protein pack off his chin. "I know why the Thuzerians never joined your strength to the Resistance. It is because John Starfire does not truly meet the requirements of the prophecy in your Bible. Were it so, he would have defeated the Shir, the unburned and unkilled plague." Z stands, which is saying something, after all we've been through in the last few hours. He stands and points a finger. "The Son of Stars is aboard this ship, come in the darkest mines of Shadow Sun Seven. She has crossed the gulf uncrossable, and she stands ready to journey into the darkness."

For some reason, Alsethus doesn't move. And then, she whispers, "We heard."

"You heard?"

"It is all the refugees speak of. A miracle. A new node, opening around them, the first new node made since the first Jorians. And a new Saint. The children are those who witnessed it." And she starts quoting. "'And the children shall bear witness, many, each pure testimony a new atom in the molecules of the Lord's plan.'" And then, in half a whisper, "'The children shall be the change, and the change shall be the children.'"

I guess I shouldn't tell her that it was the same Shadow Sun Seven node, just that Jaqi *moved* it somehow. A new node sounds more miraculous.

"Adept Taltus was cast out of our ruling council five years ago for demanding that we turn against John

Starfire for denying the scriptures. We didn't dare fight the Resistance, for we are no friends of the Empire. But now ... can I see her? The girl?"

"There will be many who wish to see her," Z says. "You may have to form a queue."

22

Jaqi

LOTS OF PEOPLE HAVE tried to come see me. The nurses turn someone away every couple of minutes. "She is resting." "She has performed great feats, yes." "Yes, she already has a copy of the Bible." "I do not think it is wise to give her any supplemental reading right now."

The Thuzerians believe a potential Saint needs her rest, which is a fine idea. Also good, I reckon, as I've been eating all the fresh bread and sweet nut paste they can bring. Probably best to keep folk out when the Chosen Oogie's got crumbs in her bed.

This time, my bone-masked nurse—being a nurse, his mask exposes most of his face save the nose—says, "I am very sorry, Sa—miss Jaqi, but this is one of the seven."

"The seven?"

"Those who went into the heart of hell, and returned with the prisoners," the nurse says. "Yourself, Adept Taltus, God honor his memory, the cross, the children, and two Zarra, God honor the memory of she who fell."

I notice he don't mention Scurv. I reckon our famous friend must be keeping a low profile as, if the holos told it even half correctly, vi killed one of them Saints.

"The surviving Zarra is here. Ah . . ." He frowns at his datapad. "Zarag-a . . ."

"Just call him Z," I say. "Let the big slab in." I've been hoping to see him. Glad he survived. And time to give him a piece of my mind.

Z comes around the curtain. At least . . . I think it's Z, but he en't got no tattoos! And no scars—that puckered scar from the poison sting has gone. He's got new, ice-white skin smooth as a babe's. Same build. Same frown. Whole new skin! "Slab! What is this? You starting over on them tattoos?"

He sits on the bed. Don't look at me. Reaches out and pages through a couple of buttons on my monitor, like he's checking my vitals, but I know my vitals is fine, and I know as much as he knows about blood, he en't a medical sort.

"Z? You thinking about blood and honor again? Forget to talk?"

He speaks, and even his voice sounds different, like he got a new throat. "Suits."

"Say what?"

"They found Suits inside of me. Microscopic Suits."

"Oh. Nano-Suits? Like what took down the Vanguard ship?"

He grunts. I reckon that's what goes for a yes among the Zarra.

I sit there trying to think of a thing to say, but he speaks up. "They heal my hurts, the doctors say. They are better able to speed my body's processes—clotting, growing new skin, healing bones—purging poison."

"That's how you came through that explosion—" Hang on. "You reckon the *Suits* healed you back on the moon of Trace?"

"They must have. I told them not to interfere with me. I told them the knowledge in my head was my people's alone, and they—they—" He starts to talk. In his Zarra language. I en't ever heard it before. It's low and guttural and has a lot of snorts and snarls and sounds like he's about to let loose a coughing fit. "All has changed, and my honor has been stripped, cast away into space. Ancestors wait at the River of Stars, but I cannot call there. Not when my body is violated."

I want to answer, but this is crazing news to me.

It weren't me did the miracle.

All that time, all that messing with the nodes, a near-impossible thing I done, and I wasn't a miracle worker?

Here I am, having done another miracle, only to find out the first one weren't really it.

"How can I bear this?" He stands, sits down again. "They violate our world, and they violate our bodies—"

"You're alive, slab," I say, and reach out to run a hand over his soft skin. Real soft, brand new. "Without you, them seven thousand people we saved would still be dying in them mines. That's enough."

"It is not enough simply to live, Jaqi. I must live with honor."

"En't there honor in just living? Just fighting on through?"

He thinks for a moment. "No."

"You're hopeless." I can't help a chuckle. "Guess Araskar was right."

"You knew?" Z tenses up like he's about to fight me—but just glares. "You knew! You knew I was dishonored!"

"Didn't know a thing, Z," I snap. "Just something Araskar said."

"What has he to offer this?"

"That whether or not I done a miracle, I had to act like a miracle worker."

Z don't seem to have an answering thought for that. I feel relieved, a bit. Oh, sure, I done some funny things with a node, but maybe I en't no miracle worker after all. Maybe there en't such a thing. Scary to think, but good all at once.

"I must return to Trace. I must challenge the Engineer and see why he has done such a thing."

"Hold on now. You en't going to go get yourself killed picking a fight with a planet full of Suits, Z." I get up out of the bed, despite the way the hospital gown blows freely around my starkers. "Kalia read me Araskar's report on Shadow Sun Seven. You could have gotten out. You could have kept X alive. And without them Suits inside you, you would have died. Araskar would have too. Way I see it, you were doing your best to get killed, here when I told you to stay alive!"

"The Faceless Butcher—" Z starts to say.

"Heard about that too. Reckon you owed him quite a debt. But Araskar was right. You had a mission."

Z don't say a thing.

"Should have stuck to the mission, if you cared about our Reckoning."

"Yes."

"Okay." I sit back down on the bed, brush some crumbs off the spot next to me, and pat it. "I'm gonna be heated with you for a bit, Z, but I want you to sit here anyway and keep me some company. I can think of a few ways to take our minds off miracles and honor and—"

"No."

"What?"

"Jaqi, you are right." Here's a thing I never thought I'd see. The big slab is ready to cry. "I have no honor. I do not even understand honor. I am a child. I have learned nothing from the time when I was pit-fighting, thinking that only in battle can I find honor."

"Now Z, I didn't say all that."

"I must go. I am truly sorry. You are a shining soul, Jaqi. A true Jorian come again, and may the galaxy have rest from pain by your gifts. Do not give into despair, in the dark days coming."

"Z—don't run off!"

"I must."

"En't you learned anything? You can just live! Don't need to go."

But in the time it takes me to say that, he's gone. I'm left staring at the curtain.

A few minutes later, I hear one of the nurses turn someone away, with a snap of, "No, she is tired, and she does not do miracles on command!"

Sure don't.

––––––––

Araskar

It's a good thing the Thuzerians have a nice hospital facility. I get even more synthskin over the burns, some gel-grown tissue replacing the parts of myself I broiled away.

I must have more synthskin than the real stuff now.

It's a lot of work to preserve a grunt like me. They treat me like an actual sentient, not something vat-cooked.

The Thuzerians also have a tranquilizer that puts me down for a good seventeen hours. It's the most sleep I've had, ever.

When I wake, the ship is still crossing the nightside of their planet, with the scattered lights of population centers dotting the darkness below, like clustered stars, reflecting the sky.

I lie in my bed, in what I guess is a long-term patient room, my face pressed against the window.

Down there, seven thousand refugees are being sorted, fed, clothed, cleaned. For once, my actions have resulted in lives lived, instead of lives lost. For once, this was about civilians saved, not slugs, not soldiers, but civilians. I spent so long trying to protect my own battalion and failing, it's a funny feeling to have succeeded at this.

Seven thousand.

Funny things, numbers. Over the thousand-year lifespan of the Second Empire, eighteen trillion crosses died fighting in the Dark Zone, taking heavily armed dreadnoughts to destroy Shir nests, to use planet-crackers and dark bombs and techno-viruses to try and kill those monsters, whatever they are.

And then John Starfire, with a force of maybe a few hundred thousand, put a stop to that. Promised us something like peace.

Now he's well on his way to killing every human in the galaxy. Three trillion humans in the galaxy, and seven thousand is but a tiny sliver of that. There'll be other bluebloods, hidden in other dark spots like Shadow Sun Seven. There'll be mass graves, whole empty corners of space filled with corpses.

There'll be new Shir nests, soon enough, springing from the Dark Zone into the wild worlds. Millions of new Shir.

All because we had to have one. A Chosen One.

One. Just one. We want to think that one person in this galaxy of ten trillion sentients can change something. I think that says less about the Son of Stars than about people in general.

Hang on. I hear something—no, I feel something. A faint stirring of strings, and winds, a faint symphony rising in the distance, a few crackling electric notes.

My door opens.

"Yes?" I roll over, wincing at the fresh pain in my leg.

"Araskar?"

"Jaqi?" I sit up. "Didn't expect you."

She closes the door. "You didn't feel me coming through that music you always going on about?"

"A bit," I say. "But I thought you would be—I don't know, with the kids, or with . . ." I don't say *with Z.*

She creeps closer, stops halfway across the room. "Hope no one's expecting me. I'm trying to sneak around. May be the last sneaking around I ever do, what with being famous."

I wait. She'll keep talking; that's how she is. It's nice to hear her voice, after so many times clutching a soulsword and listening for it. Nicer to hear the music, sweeping over me with her this close.

"Salutes." She sits down on the bed next to me.

"Salutes."

"They done released me from the hospital, gave me a room, and I think they figure I'll stay put, but I needed to do some thinking." She catches a look out the window. "En't that pretty! Look right there."

We're crossing the terminator line; below, night shades into day on a vast ocean, a wide blue thing dotted with brown and green islands, covered in a feathering of cloud.

"Would be nice to get down there, breathe some real air and eat some real matter." She sits back.

"Oh, yeah. I bet a lot of that's agricultural. Apples and potatoes, and chickens in pens eating all the protein that's not fit for the planetside. They'll serve you up a nice crispy bird, and plenty of vegetables on the side."

"Quit making me slobber." The music shifts, yearning with slow sweeps of deep stringed instruments. "I can't go down there without getting all worshipped and nonsense."

"I might have something to eat."

I reach into the pockets of the coat I wore—just an everyday, normal coat the Matakas provided, now rather singed—and fish out the crumpled, partially melted remains of the Routalais chocolate I bought on Shadow Sun Seven.

"I'm sure it got damaged in the explosion," I say. "But I figure you and the kids would like the chocolate."

She snatches it out of my hand. "Slab! You didn't!" She breaks off a bit of it and starts chewing on it, winces as she realizes the wrapper has melted partially into the chocolate. "That's fantastic. It must have gotten all fixed back up after it melted."

"Not any worse for having gone through a pit fight, and an explosion? And near-vacuum? Also I bled on it."

"Quiet, Araskar, I'm living in this moment. Mmm." She keeps chewing, and stops, then says, "Oh, I'm sorry. You have some. Reckon you earned it."

"I'm okay," I say.

"What? Araskar, you been through hell and back a few times. You deserve a little something nice. What's your garbled mouth taste like now? Blood?"

"Synthskin, actually."

"Well, if you got the choice, why en't you tasting chocolate?" She laughs, breaks off a piece and hands it to me.

I have to admit, it tastes damn good, even with the bits of the wrapper. The taste lingers in the mouth, and it'll shade everything for the next few days. I may have a few good days, for the first time in a while.

"Finest thing in the whole universe, this," she mutters through a mouthful. We eat in silence, then she says, "I'm leaving afore we make planetfall. Might have to steal one of them fancy ships, but I reckon Scurv and I en't no strangers to that."

"What? Why?"

"Reason you gave me back on Trace, slab. Gotta figure out what's going on in the Dark Zone. Scurv says there's a planet and star in there the devils don't disturb. Vi can show me the coordinates, and I can find the node, what with the star-map the Suits decrypted." She eats more chocolate, chewing in the silence. "You were right, slab."

"Right about what?"

"I en't no miracle worker, but I got to act like it. It was Suits who healed Z back on the moon of Trace."

"Suits?" I suppose it makes sense now, since he's become unkillable. Something has to live inside him, restoring him like that. "Nano-Suits. But how'd they get inside him? I mean, wouldn't he have noticed?"

"They're tiny. Crawled in his ear or some such."

"Still." I can't help remembering the order of things. Z was nearly dead of poison on the planet Trace. Then he did die, on the moon. Back on Shadow Sun Seven, after he was shocked insensate, he was back up on his feet within a few minutes.

And I remember what Jaqi did with the sword. I remember how it felt.

Felt like a miracle.

Though I don't say that. "Don't be so sure."

"Slab, I en't sure about anything anymore. But it feels good. Feel a bit free now. I en't the special oogie. But I can figure out what John Starfire knows. I reckon if we're going to find some clue, something that makes sense of all this, it'll be there. The devils leave the place alone for a reason."

"A reason Scurv knows?"

"Vi en't exactly wordy on that."

"But you trust vim."

"I think vi understands why John Starfire went bad, why we have to stop this crazing before the Resistance can kill most of the galaxy."

"I should go with you."

"I need you to stay here, slab, for a couple of reasons. One is that you got plenty of intel in your brainpan about what the Chosen One—or I figure he's the Usurper now—is up to. The other is that I want you here, packed in with a batch of sword-wielding Thuzerians, because I reckon now you been seen elsewhere, John Starfire and half the galaxy going to come for you."

"Well." I snatch a piece of chocolate out of her hands, and she glares, grabs for it. I play a little game of keep-a-way, her reaching for it, me holding it just out of reach. "Come on, how will you kill John Starfire if you can't steal some chocolate back?"

She smacks my face playfully, then snatches it out of my hand. "Just like that, slab. I learned this in them pit fights."

"Easy. I don't need any more scars."

For a moment we're silent, and for a moment, I think about telling her about the music, the way it swells and soars and lifts me, and how there's something waiting for her, I know, not just a devil, though I can't say how I know.

Instead, I realize she's looking at me funny.

Shit, she probably thinks I'm about to drop a line on her, being playful like that. I'm acting like I haven't acted since Rashiya.

Can't help it. It feels good, to have done a mission for something other than death's sake. "So, ah, you have a plan for when you get to this planet?"

"No." She laughs a bit. "I en't got a clue what I'm going to do about them devils. Scurv says there's a temple there vi couldn't get into, a thing filled with secrets. All the bits that don't make it into the books."

"You have to come back," I say. "Don't leave me alone, promising everyone the real Chosen One'll be along any second now."

"You'll do well on your own, slab," she says. "Head of the Reckoning, wielding a mighty soulsword."

"Presenting a beautiful target."

"Come on now. Fella like you? I en't never seen someone so unkillable. And with them scars, there's going to be a whole batch of warrior women lining up at this door."

That leaves me speechless. "Scars?"

"A real mate don't want a lover who's too pretty."

I'm well aware now that we're just looking at each other, by the light of the planet's dawn outside, silently eating chocolate, while the music pulses softly. It's a shame she can't hear it.

"What'll you do once this is over?" she asks.

"Over? This is going to be over?"

"I have to believe it'll be, slab. I have to believe that if I just figure out this miracle business, and this Dark Zone, and take out John Starfire, I'll get something like a normal life. Then I can learn that reading, and see some nice shows, and drink some of the good booze and maybe even something like a family . . ." Her voice falls. "It'll be someone else's time to fight, once we're done. That crazing talk?"

"Not crazing," I say.

"You wish for that too?"

"I've never thought of it that way." I hold up the last piece of my chocolate. "In my experience, all the good things in life are like this. Your memories might be the reason someone kills you. Might as well enjoy the moment, and make the memory good."

She does't say anything to that. Now that's unusual. I wonder whether I offended her. Hard to tell by the low beat of the music—

And then she kisses me.

I haven't been kissed by anyone, ever, save Rashiya. Jaqi's different—hungrier, less familiar—but she breaks it off after a minute, turns away, says, "Sorry."

"Why sorry?"

"Oh, seemed like the thing to do in the moment, and—well—damn it, Araskar, I'm about to go face them devils again, and I don't see how I'm supposed to come out alive, and maybe you could just indulge a girl a bit?"

"Indulge." I didn't think I was so easy to stun into silence. "Indulge you?"

"You know!"

"I get what you mean, I just—I thought you hated me."

"I en't never been picky!"

Well, that's . . . It takes me a minute to think of what to say, a minute in which the silence grows more pronounced. "That's quite an endorsement," I say with a forced laugh.

"So . . . you saying no."

"No. I mean, I'm saying yes." Damn, in my short life I doubt I've ever sounded this stupid. "I'd be glad to indulge you. I can't say I've had much experience, truth."

"For a fella so good at fighting, you ought to know the importance of coming on strong." She lifts her shirt off. "I just want you to help me forget there's a morning."

I take off my own shirt, showing whole maps of scars. She touches my scars, each one. I touch her smooth skin. Slowly, just growing used to the idea of touching each other.

We were never made to love.

Never made to live.

But tonight, we do both.

Jaqi thinks I don't hear her leaving. She doesn't know I've been awake most of the night, just listening to her breathing, feeling the gentle rise and fall of her shoulder blades.

I watch as she rolls out of bed, grunts and throws on her clothes, mutters something as she takes a sip of water from the bag hung next to the door.

And I watch the figure that stands outside the window. Floating right there in the vacuum, her green eyes piercing me through the clear plasticene, her red hair drifting in zero gravity. She lifted one callused hand, presses it against the window.

No. I turn my head away, look into the darkness. *No, I don't want to die anymore.*

It's a strange feeling.

And beautiful.

So this is living.

———————

Jaqi

I make a seal check around the outside of the shuttle while Scurv examines the cockpit. Shuttle was due to take folk down to the planet; they will think we're just another load of refugees, and we'll be through the node before they're the wiser.

Then I hear the voice say, "You aren't leaving without us."

Kalia says it with a smile, and I reckon I smile back. It is good to see them. I thought it best to sneak off, but truth is, I en't got the strength to go into another risky situation like this without seeing the reason for it one more time.

The kids have been scrubbed, and look clean, well-dressed, the sorts of clothes they ought to be wearing. I feel strange, embracing them, as I still look a space scab, with my frizzy hair and my shipboard scrubs. I'll always look the part of a spaceways scab, no matter what miracles I make. "Aiya, gonna miss you kids."

"This is the whole reason we had that map!" Kalia says, from where she's tucked her head against my neck. "Let us see it!"

I laugh a little, look over my shoulder at Scurv, who is giving the shuttle a once-over. "Would have been nice if someone told us that ahead of time."

"Jaqi," Kalia says, and pulls away from me. "Please. Let me come with you."

"Kalia, I didn't take Araskar—or Z, for that matter, why'd you think I'd take you?" I knew she'd have plenty of reasons, so I go and cut her off. "Your uncle needs you. Your brother needs you. Stay here. Guide them. The trouble en't over, not a bit."

"Jaqi, you can't even read those prophecies! I—" She stops. "I think there's something dangerous waiting for you. I've read the prophecies over and over, and I think that this is when the Children of Giants—"

"There's plenty of dangerous things waiting for me on this mission." I kneel down, pull Toq in my arms one more time, and signal for her to come here as well. "I got you here, all right? Now your uncle and them other refugees are going to need your help. They got to make their case to the rest of the galaxy, help the worlds see what John Starfire done wrong, turn the worlds against him." Swez's words come on back to me. "Most folk en't thinking beyond their next check, and what makes it easier to cut that check. They en't going to make a fuss if them bluebloods are gone. You need to make them listen, aiya? Make them see there's more to worry about than what's for dinner. You been through hell and back. You got words to say."

She doesn't answer. After a moment, she says, "Okay, well, promise me you'll take the Bible."

She shoves her own copy of the book at me, all ragged with her notes and folded pages. I hold it up, looking between her and this book. "Am I going to ask Scurv to read it to me?" I say. "Come on now."

"Please take it."

I don't want to, but I do. Hell. This'll be the death of me afore I even learn the words in it.

23

Jaqi

"WE RECOMMEND YOU OPEN YOUR EYES."

"One second now, slab."

I'm enjoying the memory. Araskar kisses me again, and I groan and moan, cuz that just makes the slack better, and he rolls over, puts a hand in the small of my back, and it's so good, so sweet, I don't ever want to leave that room and don't ever want to leave the feel of his bare skin, of my chest pressing against the scars on his—

"Look, Jaqi."

"En't nothing to see." But I do so anyway.

There, in front of the viewscreen, is nothing.

Darkness millions of light years in every direction, nothing but darkness, filling the universe, a darkness full of things darker and deeper and more monstrous than any nightmare you ever done had.

A thousand suns and planets swallowed up in there, turned into nurseries for those nightmares.

Here we sit. In our stolen shuttle. On a dark node, one

of them I used to use to hide out. This node en't far from Bill's, in truth; probably about as far from where I grew up as two star systems is from each other.

"I was having a nice daydream, slab."

"Was it about us?" Scurv has taken to flirting with me.

"Ask again after we done finished this mission," I say. Scurv en't a bad slab vimself, but I find I been looking forward to Araskar again. Once life done turned back to normal.

Scurv sits in the co-captain's chair, and lights a cigar, smells awful foul and probably far against regulation to smoke on the ship. "You going to kill us doing that," I say, while vi sucks away on the rolled-up stick.

"Which is more dangerous, a smoke, or a jump into the Dark Zone blind?"

"How about both?" I say.

"Ah, that being the case, we are waiting on you."

I nearly gag on vir smoke, and think about how nice it would have been to breathe real planetside air on the Thuzerian planet, and then I think there's probably real air on this planet, this TS-101.

If I can only make the jump through Hell itself.

"Okay. So we'll go."

This is it. The Chosen Girl going to do the dumbest damn thing she ever done Chosen to do.

I reach out for the node, and pure space pulls at us,

and I think on that node coordinate we got for TS-101, and I don't think about deep, dark space, about a planet-sized face with jagged spurs of teeth and tentacles could squeeze the life out of a gas giant, about furnaces inside them Shir where stolen stars burn, I just think about Araskar's hand when it traced the bones of my neck, I just think on that, as we go into pure space . . .

And out . . .

Takes a real long time before I open my eyes.

One single star sits in the sky—a good-sized yellow sun, sort of nice normal sun you see in tourist brochures for vacation planets.

All around it, darkness. Not a star to be seen. Nightmares for light-years.

One single planet, green oceans, brown dots of land, shifting masses of cloud, in the darkness, sitting right above us.

One planet, and one sun. Here in the center of the Dark Zone.

"You told me the truth," I gasp.

"You think we would feed us to the devil?"

I let out a breath so long and ragged that I end up hacking and coughing. Scurv's lit another one of them smokes, and vi's staring at the monitor.

"That's it, it is. We were there a year, trying to get into the temple." Vi leans forward, programs a set of coordinates and landing information into the shuttle. "And now we go back."

"What makes you think we can get in now? Think it'll be any different?" I ask.

"We have the Son of Stars with us, ai?" Scurv takes a long drag off the smoke.

"I en't no Chosen Thing."

"Do not disparage our faith, Chosen Thing."

We fly toward the planet.

A thousand years of fighting in the Dark Zone has produced a ring of debris, orbiting far out beyond the planet where a moon would be, had this planet a moon. Instead, a silvery thread runs through space, bits of wreckage miles apart. The sensors speak, give me a running list of what's out there, what's settled into orbit here in their mechanical voice. Metal and plasticene. And organic matter. Bodies, the sensors explain. Dead crosses, a good million of them, forming a ring. No danger to us, as space is big and we've got a good sense-field.

I'm flying past the wreckage of ten thousand Shir battles.

"Sobering," Scurv says. Vi reads the screen, even though I've set it to read the relevant material aloud to me. "Says there's about a billion corpses out there. And them only a fraction of what's died in the Dark Zone over the years."

"Makes you realize why old John Starfire got so popular."

Scurv finishes that stinking cigarillo. "The people see what the screens want them to see, aiya? The Empire hid these deaths from folk. John Starfire hides those miners from folk. What will your Reckoning keep off the screens?"

"Nothing, ai, and you can put that lip right out the airlock," I say.

Scurv just laughs.

Well, vi was an asshole in most of them holos, if I remember right. Didn't lie about that.

But the Reckoning en't going to have dirty laundry to hide. The Oogie of Stars has decided on that.

We enter the planet's atmosphere. The heat of reentry swallows the ship, and then suddenly we're in the rushing wind and wet clouds of upper atmos, and then there's a dark ocean beneath us. We reach the coast of a big landmass; it's all wild, tangled forests of big black trees, clinging to the rocks, wide muddy river deltas, not a sign of a sentient-built thing in sight. Kind of planet folk dream about finding, a place untouched by thousands of years, where life's taken a new tack.

Except no—I start to notice a few shapes, under the trees. I think I see a bit of a wall, and a tower, but they're eaten by vines, and crowded with flying things, and screaming animals bellow from the woods around them.

"What do you reckon this was?" I ask.

"If we interpreted the words we read right, this was one of the first outposts in our galaxy." Vi pauses to take another foul breath off that nasty smoke. "Terraformed by the First Empire, during the golden age of Jorian and human. This temple, where we take you—we cannot be sure, but we think, inside there, might be a node to Earth."

"That's crazing talk, right out of myth."

"Is it?" Scurv says. "Do you not feel? Part of us is still cross, and we feel it."

Scurv says it, and then I realize I can sense it. And it's—oh hell, it's music. Just like Araskar done talked about. Soaring music, furious music, notes like I en't ever heard, and at the center of it all, that song my mother done sung, the one I heard when I healed Z. *Bend, pull, bend, pull.* Just a field song, but so much more. Wrapping around me, swallowing me, just like when I held that sword over Z, just like when I pulled that node toward us outside Shadow Sun Seven.

"And here it be."

Jutting out into the ocean, connected to the mainland by a causeway, is this massive complex. There's a wide round wall around some sort of building, definitely a Jorian building, crystalline glass and steel rising in layers, one on the other. The spun-glass that indicates a Jorian structure, but bigger, more complex than any I ever seen, woven into a metal structure. In a circle around the walls, standing in the ocean waves, are thirteen crystal statues, each of a figure, holding a soulsword out into the sky.

Each one wears armor and a helmet the likes of which I en't imagined; all curves and twists, like a living thing. Each one has a face like they done seen the most beautiful of all things the galaxy has to offer. Now *these* folk look like Sons of Stars and Special Oogies.

"The first Jorians," Scurv says.

"That's them?"

"That en't nothing but stone-glass, but that's what they looked like. Here we go."

We land on the causeway in front of this place, and I step out. The atmos smells fresher and finer than anything I ever smelled; it's wild and thick with the salt air of the ocean, and I smell a bit of a sense-field, something protecting this temple.

"We tried to find a way in for ages," Scurv says.

Together, Scurv and I walk up to the temple gates. They're covered with plants, half torn down, but I see the sense-field, sure enough, and it's a nasty, buzzing thing, sort of thing meant to kill anyone trips and falls against it. The lock sure looks like it's a thousand years old. Just a scan-box, set into the wall, with a plasticene cover gone cracked and half crumbled after so long.

"Made to scan the right sort of DNA," vi says. "Try sticking your hand in."

"You think it'll just open for me? That's crazing."

"Is you the Son of Stars, or isn't you?" Scurv asks, the lit smoke trailing from vir mouth.

All right, then.

I stick my hand into the scan box.

Something groans, and the apparatus roars, and the sense-field vanishes.

Well, shit.

The temple stands open to me.

That—that damn near proves I *am* this chosen whady-athink. Who'd have imagined such a thing? It's crazing, crazing Dark, and don't that seem more apt than ever.

"We go inside?" I say. A rotted pathway, covered in roots and shrubs, leads up to the building. I step in—and the sense-field pops back up, between Scurv and I.

"Aw, hell!"

Scurv groans, and pulls out one of them pistols and shoots, but the green shard just breaks to bits, scatters across the field, and vi shrugs, says something I can't make out over the buzzing. I look around for some lock that'll undo the sense-field out here. Nothing. I reckon I need the main controls, in the building.

Separated from Scurv. Vi's on the other side of the

field looking like a lost kitten.

Vi yells things I can't make out through the field. I shrug. What can I do? I look around for some way to deactivate the field from in here, but I reckon that when this place was people it must have been keyed, and them controls are in the main building.

I turn and walk to this temple.

Didn't think Scurv would make a stupid mistake like that, getting locked out.

After picking my way along the overgrown pathway, I get finally to a curved entryway, which leads me into an antechamber. There ought to be plenty of animals and bugs in here, if I understand planets with real matter, but that sense-field done kept them out, so it's overgrown with fungus and vines, but at the end of the chamber, there's another door and—

The music rises. Triples, roars, beats at me like something physical, knocks me to my knees. My eyes water. My mind's gone mad, gone empty, and I hear Z's voice come floating through, each word carried by a surge of music sounds like it comes from a thousand-instrument orchestra.

The Starfire is the fuel that burns in pure space. The original Jorians could touch it, and did great miracles with it, and made the nodes so that the other races could spread across the stars. Humans grafted their idea of a God onto the

Starfire, but it is an older, greater force.

When I can see, I see light pulsing from the chamber beyond. Light, moving in time with the music. And I walk toward it—or maybe I'm carried.

And then I'm there, and I'm in the light, and I see—

"Come to me."

"Mama?"

That's my mother! She's smiling at me, showing them big teeth I remember, and her dark skin is shining with a sheen of sweat, just like it did after a long day picking in the fields—"Mater, that's you!"

I reach out for her, but I touch only music. The notes sift through my hands, dance along my arms up to my ears.

"Come to me."

"Papa?" There he is, with that curly, gray-touched hair, that broken tooth showing in his smile—he never told me how he done broke that tooth, did he?

"Papa, Mama, I thought the Empire done shot you off the side of some scow! You're here! You're alive! I knew you had a life, I knew you mattered."

Papa reaches out to embrace me and—I touch only music. Notes swirl up my reach, swirl around my mind, scatter at my feet.

The light wraps around me, and then suddenly, it lifts away from me, and I'm standing here on a thin walkway, in a vast, empty chamber, reaching far into the earth, music roaring in deep, vibrating rhythms around me.

"Mama, Papa?" They're here? Did I walk into some kind of heaven? "Answer me!"

They reappear for a second, formed out of swirls of music. And now they're looking at me funny. "You're her," they say together.

"Of course I'm her." Am I crying? I can't tell. "It's Jaqi! You done—you done come back! I waited. I waited for you to come back. I waited at Bill's, for so long, and he told me maybe you was all right, but he didn't reckon so—"

Oh, how I waited, how I wanted to see them come back in through the airlock doors.

"I waited for you to come," they say, together.

And somehow their faces change—they're almost my parents' faces, but they swirl together, and it's like a vast, whirling set of features, formed of swirls of music—a face that could swallow a whole planet—

I stagger back. This en't my parents. "You're the devil!"

The music shifts, moves away from me, a living thing now. <u>I waited for you.</u>

How can this be? How can I be here, in this music, with my parents, and I see the devil? "You're the devil?"

<u>Not the devil.</u>

It en't lying. This *thing*—whatever it is, it's is one of

them devils and it en't, as they was just cold and whispering voices, but this is whole soaring suites of music, music that's hit me hard enough to see Mama and Papa alive again, even though I know they's gone for good.

And suddenly something changes. The thing—whatever it is, whether it be Shir, music, my parents, this thing that's trying to talk to me—it runs, disappearing into the darkness below me, and the music fades in my ears, and I'm left standing on the walkway, and I'm facing—

I'm facing a man.

I don't know him, but he's familiar. Where've I seen this scab before? A brown beard, peppered with gray, an arm gleaming with a little bit of the steel-and-synth-skin that was in Araskar's leg, and a soulsword. His hand clutches and unclutches the soulsword.

I know this scab's face. I seen it—I seen it somewhere, on the news—

No.

"Not the devil you know," says John Starfire.

To be concluded in:
The Starfire Trilogy Book Three
Memory's Blade

Acknowledgments

The second book is a real mindf*ck, to quote the philosopher.

Again, huge thanks are due to Beth Meacham, editor of editors, for light but firm guidance in all matters of this trilogy, and to Sara Megibow, agent of agents, for getting it out there. Big thanks are due as well to Katharine and Mordicai at Tor.com for publicity, and Beth Cato, Mary Robinette Kowal, and Wendy Wagner for cover quotes and signings. SPACE BUGS!

Once again, a dump truck of THANK YOU to Langley Hyde who read a very early draft and wisely told me how to BIGGERIFY the space adventure to have more and more adventure, more verve, and a better character journey. The cool parts are all her fault, y'all.

Thanks to the friends who've kept me sane during the Battle of the Trilogy, with special credit to Effie Seiberg, Jessica and Brian Holdaway, Cory Skerry, Sean Patrick Kelley, Joey Elmer, Rebecca Mablango-Mayor, and my wonderful coworkers and students at Northwest Indian College.

All credit and love to my family, starting with my father, mother, brothers, and sisters, who have been constant supports and sounding boards. Most love of all to Chrissy, Adia, Sam, and Brigitta, whose love burns so bright I can't see without it.

About the Author

Photograph by Chrissy Ellsworth

SPENCER ELLSWORTH's short fiction has previously appeared in *Lightspeed, The Magazine of Fantasy & Science Fiction,* and *Tor.com.* He is the author of the Starfire trilogy, which begins with *Starfire: A Red Peace.* He lives in the Pacific Northwest with his wife and three children, works as a teacher/administrator at a small tribal college on a Native American reservation, and blogs at spencerellsworth.com.

TOR·COM

Science fiction. Fantasy. The universe.

And related subjects.

*

More than just a publisher's website, *Tor.com*
is a venue for **original fiction, comics,** and
discussion of the entire field of SF and fantasy,
in all media and from all sources. Visit our site
today—and join the conversation yourself.